I Think We're Alone Now

Virginia Guido

*In memory of my son, Frankie Guido,
whose appreciation for the macabre inspired
me to create these stories.*

Table of Contents*

*AKA Twisted Tunes of Terror

WELCOME TO MY NIGHTMARE

Even as a little girl growing up in Brooklyn, I was both frightened and fascinated by things that "go bump in the night". The house my mother rented was behind a three-story walk-up. In order to visit us, you had to go through the hallway of that building. In other words, you had to love us to make that trip to our house. I did not even have a window with a view of the street until we moved.

The house was rife with doors opening on their own, lights that would go on and off for no reason, and sounds of footsteps in the stairwell. Things seemed to always be moving around my dresser at night. Maybe it was a child's weird imagination; maybe it wasn't. However, when you're a little girl, you tend to believe these things are real.

When I was twelve, my mother bought a brownstone, also in Brooklyn. When I looked out the bedroom window, I was excited to see the sidewalks, other houses, cars, and kids playing. But I wasn't as thrilled at having a constant thumping noise from the ceiling over my head at night (see *Unforgettable*), or witnessing objects slide off the furniture and crash to the floor.

The worst experience I had in that house was with my Siamese cat and the creaking floor. The house was old, with wood floors that would "settle", either from the heat or the cold. The trouble with this was the direction of the creaking sound. The noise would start at the door to my room, travel past my bed, and into my mother's room. My cat would follow the sound by looking in that direction, stretching her neck as it entered my mother's room. Then she would turn to me with a look as if to say, "Didn't you see THEM?"

From that point on, I never went upstairs to bed without that cat held out in front of me!

No matter where I lived, I've always had the feeling of not being alone, that something or someone (an entity or spirit) was with me. Now that I'm older, I'm positive it's my dearly departed family members.

Still, I have difficulty sleeping at night; the stories I write are from my dreams. They are vivid and eerie. I wake up afraid and unable to go back to sleep until I write them down.

Please note: each story shares its title with a song (no copyright infringement). I got that idea from watching *Grey's Anatomy (*see Acknowledgements*)*. It's now my thing, too.

So, dear reader, as you peruse each story, you are entering my mind, my thoughts, and my nightmares.

Welcome to the other side!

ALMOST PARADISE

Jessica noticed the foliage around her seemed to sparkle as she walked through the park. The path was so bright, almost luminous, and the chirping of the birds made the sweet sound of wind chimes on a breezy day. She pivoted her head from side to side as she took inventory of her surroundings. Everything was so crystal clear!

The scenery reminded her of a View-Master toy she had when she was a child. She could look through the lenses at the pictures, and the images on the disc would seem to jump off the screen. Here, a place hidden in time, the environment appeared to come alive and grow closer to her as she traveled down the glittering road.

Not far from her, Jessica saw a young man sitting on a bench feeding some kind of birds. *Was he there all this time?* She approached him and sat beside him. He said nothing but continued to toss shiny nuggets to silver peacock-like birds strutting around the bench. Finally, he looked up and acknowledged her. "Hey," he said with a smile.

Jessica returned the smile, "Hey to you."

"My name is Michael."

"I'm Jessica."

"Been here long?"

"What do you mean by 'here'? This bench or the park?"

"Park? You think this is a park?"

"Listen to me, Michael. I'm confused, captivated, and a little scared. So please don't play games with me."

"A park would be the ideal place to play games if this place really were a park."

Jessica sighed. "So this is not a park. Maybe it's a garden or some kind of tourist attraction that I've wandered into by accident."

"Did you wander in here, Jessica?"

"I'm not sure how I got here, but I'm glad I've had the opportunity to experience such a magical place. The air is crisp and clean; the colors are vibrant. Everything is so brilliant, it actually hurts my eyes. Tell me, Michael, how did you get here?"

"Me? I've been here since the beginning. You just never noticed me before today. You were so busy living your life, making your plans, and doing your thing, you never saw me. But I saw you. Every single day, I watched you."

Jessica was shocked. "Why waste your time watching me? I'm an average person, nothing special."

Michael laughed, "Oh, Jessica, don't sell yourself short. You are an extraordinary woman, worthy of my observation."

"But there's nothing special to see in me." Jessica shook her head and started to rise. "Perhaps I should just move along, so I don't catch whatever it is that is making you quite insane."

"Where will you go?"

"Any place where I can find people who are like me."

"Then, sweet Jessica, you have definitely come to the right place. Everyone here is exactly like you: remarkable!"

Jessica raised her eyebrows. "And just what is it that makes me remarkable in your eyes?"

"Ah! She wants a list. Okay, here is your list. You have shown patience to those who could never be rushed. You give so much of yourself and your time that you have no time to call your own. You genuinely care about people, even those who do not care about you. And you worry about everything–not about things that can affect you, but things that could affect others."

"Big deal. Lots of people are like that. You should take some time to watch them and learn."

"I did watch them, and I learned that they need a place like this as a reward for putting others before themselves."

"So, this place is…Heaven? Am I dead?" Jessica put her hand on her chest to feel the reassuring beating of her heart.

Michael chuckled, "No, this is not Heaven, and you are still very much alive."

Jessica furrowed her brow. "Okay, I give up. Where am I?"

"Quite some time ago, I came into a huge sum of money. I have no family and I needed nothing, so I created this place. It's not Heaven, but it *is* a haven. A spa of sorts, for good people to reside."

Michael continued, "I looked on the internet for 'people who perform good deeds' and discovered many unselfish people like you, Jessica. They also have no family anymore, but rather than wallow in self-pity, they choose to give of themselves. In other words, they have channeled their grief into good works.

"If you decide to stay, all the things you have denied yourself will be here at your beck and call: plays you have missed because you donated your ticket money, books you had no time to read, and culinary delights you could never afford."

Jessica was stunned. "How long can I stay here?"

"Stay as long as you like. No one has left…yet. I imagine the only reason for leaving would be if you pass away. And I would be prepared to make your final exit as pleasant and blessed as possible. So, Jessica, will you stay?...Jessica, can you hear me? Jessica?"

Jessica slowly opened her eyes and looked around at all the faces surrounding her. *Why is everyone staring at me? How did I get on the floor? What's going on?*

A tuxedo-clad man holding a microphone said, "Jessica Darling…Miss Darling? You just won the lottery! It's our biggest jackpot ever! You passed out as soon as you reached the stage. Are you okay? Here, take my hand. Let me help you up."

She shook her head to clear it. "Yes, yes, I'm fine, thank you."

"Do you have any family with you?"

"No, I have no family. I'm the only one left."

"Well," the host looked out over the audience and flashed a dazzling white smile as he spoke, "can you tell us what your plans will be now that you are rich beyond belief?"

Jessica leaned into the microphone and whispered, "I do have a plan…for the most extraordinary people on earth."

BREAK ON THROUGH
TO THE OTHER SIDE

"How can I get noticed by the…you know… girls?" Carl asked his father.

Abe pondered his son's question, reminiscing about his own youth. *Aah, 14-year-old blues are being sung again, this time by my son.*

"There's a talent show at your school next month, right? Why not do something so cool that…you know…those girls would find you totally awesome?"

"That could work. So, what've you got in mind for me to do?"

"Me? You're depending on me for talent ideas? Ask your mother. She was once a girl. She'll know what turns her— um, I mean, what turns a girl's head."

Walking into the garage, Carl called to his mother, "Mom, I need a fantastic act for the school's talent show. Dad said you could help."

Putting down her tools and wiping the grease from her hands, Megan looked at her son with a smile on her face. "How about something magical, like Criss Angel or David Copperfield? Illusions are the in thing. You could go dressed all in goth clothing and look very mysterious."

"That would be so cool!" Carl exclaimed. "What illusion can I do?"

"Escape artist," she replied. "You're such an expert at eluding me when chores need to be done, so imagine how great you'll be at 'escaping' for the school show."

"Ha ha, you're hilarious. Seriously, what should I do?"

Megan looked around the garage for ideas. She noticed the Halloween decorations and snapped her fingers. "There!" She pointed to a small Styrofoam coffin. "You can escape from that."

"Too small, Mom. Get real."

"What? No, I'm talking about a real coffin. Your uncle Jake is a funeral director. He can get a cheap one for us and I can install the panel to hide you."

Over the next few weeks, Carl, Megan, Abe, and Jake worked on the makeshift coffin. Carl practiced hiding behind the false panel before it was attached to the inside of the box.

When everything was in place, Jake climbed in and showed Carl how to lie in the casket, and Megan had Jake flip the panel to cover himself.

Finally, it was time for Carl to try it. He opened his eyes wide and took a deep breath. "I can't do it!"

"Come on, Carl. See how easy it is," Jake coaxed.

He shook his head. "No, I just can't get in that…that…that…thing."

"Look, we're gonna take it to the school and leave it backstage. You're already registered for the show. Maybe you'll change your mind by then." Abe was ever the optimist.

Two nights before the talent show, Elliot Spivey, the school custodian, heard some unusual sounds coming from the auditorium. He leaned closer to the vent in his office, which was adjacent to the balcony of the room in question. Nodding his head, he whispered, "Yep, there's something going on in there."

Elliot headed for the auditorium, the volume of the noise increasing as he got nearer. He looked through the glass on the door. *What the hell?* Elliot rubbed his eyes and looked again. *This is crazy. This is not happening.*

It appeared that there were lights, almost in human form, slipping out of the coffin that had been left on the stage. Elliot noticed some of the forms resembled students and teachers from bygone eras. He recognized them from their pictures on the memorial wall.

Backing away from the door, Elliot retreated to his office. He grabbed his gear and hastily left the building, muttering, "Twenty-five years of faithful service to this school still ain't worth stickin' around for this show."

Sitting in his car, he called the police.

"Good evening, Gravesend Police Department. How can I help you?"

"Please," he said, "I'm the custodian for R.U. Insidious High School. Please send a car here. Now! Please!"

The desperation in his voice sent chills down the spine of the operator. "What is the nature of your emergency, sir?"

"I can't describe this… you wouldn't believe me, anyway. Please, just send a car to the high school. I'm in the parking lot. I'll be waiting for you." Shivering, he watched the school windows, each shining with a blue-gray flickering light.

The next flash of light Elliot saw came from the green and white police car pulling into the lot.

That's odd. I thought we replaced all the green and white police cars with blue and white ones.

Still, Elliot flashed his lights to alert the police of his location. When no one left the vehicle, he got out and walked over to the car. After peering into the driver's window, Elliot backed away, but he was not quick enough to escape.

The next morning, Megan brought in the local paper and pointed to the headlines. "Look at this, Abe. The custodian from Carl's school was reported missing last night. Police found his belongings and car in the school parking lot, but no Elliot Spivey."

"So, what are they doin' about it?"

"It says here that 'Mr. Spivey had called to report strange occurrences at the school. However, the police were inexplicably delayed in responding to the call. Upon arrival, they searched the school from top to bottom and found nothing suspicious except a broken coffin on the stage.' The cops claim it was covered with scorch marks inside and out."

Megan was shaking as she picked up the phone to call her brother.

A sleepy voice mumbled, "Hello."

"Jake, tell me, and be honest, where did you get that casket we were working on for Carl?"

No answer.

"Jake, dammit, I'm serious. Where did you get it?"

"I had it in the warehouse. Found it here when I took over the business and moved it immediately because it gave me the heebie-jeebies. There was some kind of history connected to this place, but I didn't pay much attention to what the story was. Probably some urban legend started by kids at a campfire or sleepover."

"Please, we need to know."

"Listen, the guy who owned this funeral parlor was a little touched in the head, you know? He talked about a 'portal from hell' and how the 'dead were going to get him' because he 'saw their souls leaving the portal and entering the land of the living through that casket.' Crazy talk from someone who used too much embalming fluid in a poorly ventilated area."

"Well, that casket portal is gone now. Destroyed, by the looks of the pictures in today's paper. And the custodian, who may have witnessed whatever went on at the school last night, is also gone. Disappeared." Megan hung up and put her head in her hands. She didn't even hear Carl when he came down to the kitchen.

"Mom, Dad…" Carl softly said. "I have to tell you why I couldn't do that escape trick."

His parents gave their full attention to him as he continued. "It's what I saw, or what I thought I saw. Bright lights were floating out through the wooden sides of that box, one after the other."

Megan recalled that Jake had said the old man claimed the dead came back for the witnesses.

If what Jake said is true…

She was trying to sort this scenario out in her head but couldn't think straight because of all the blinding lights filling the kitchen, flying toward them, one-by-one.

CREATURES OF THE NIGHT

The bunny trembled and crouched low behind the bush. She watched furtively as the scary and mean-looking hunter crept along the path. His head swiveled from left to right as he searched for his prey in the light of the full moon.

Turning her furry head to look at the other side of the path, she saw the snake as he monitored the hunter's movements. She burrowed further down, closer to the grass, and wished she was already home. It was much too late to be out here. She was hungry and her small tummy was starting to rumble.

I must not make a sound! Neither of them has seen me, and I'd like it to stay that way.

She had encounters with these types of creatures before. They were heartless and cruel. She had been eluding the hunter all night as she witnessed the carnage he left behind. Everything was smashed and destroyed beyond recognition. She sensed his rifle might be empty as he swung it like a club to cut down anything in his path.

She surveyed the snake. *Why is he hiding? What's he waiting for?* She wanted to jump up and run as fast as she could, but she knew her white fur would practically glow in the moon's light. She couldn't call attention to herself. Silently, she kept her eyes on both creatures of the night.

Her eyes widened as she heard a sudden snap! The snake struck the hunter from behind. The scaly serpent managed to get a chokehold around the hunter's arms and bit him on the shoulder. The hunter howled in pain and dropped his rifle.

The bunny suppressed the urge to leap for joy; she didn't want to give away her hiding spot.

Releasing the hunter, the snake glared at him as he crumbled to his knees. Shaking and crying, the hunter gathered up his things and offered them to the snake.

"Please, take my candy. If this isn't enough, I'll bring more tomorrow. Just don't hurt me anymore."

"If you ever come near my sister again, I'll do more than just bite you! Tomorrow, at school, you'll return her doll, money, and lunchbox. You'll apologize to her while the whole class watches. Do you understand me? Your bullying days are over."

The hunter nodded, wiped his tears, and ran down the road without looking back. The snake bent down, took the hunter's bag of candy and toy rifle.

He looked around and called out, "Hey, Squirt, where are you? We gotta get home. Mom and Dad are probably freaking out because we're so late."

The bunny hopped out of the shadows. "Thanks, Snake. Do you really think he'll leave me alone?"

"Sure, especially since he didn't know you had an older brother. I told you that I'd take care of you. He's gonna think twice before he bothers anyone again. Plus, we got his Halloween candy as a bonus."

The bunny grinned through her painted-on whiskers. "Um, since we are already in trouble, can we go to a few more houses? I didn't get much of a chance to go trick-or-treating."

Snake put his "scaly" arm around his furry-bunny sister. "Sure, why not. You deserve some fun!"

CALENDAR GIRL

With a smile plastered on her face,
As her hands grip the heavy tray.
She watches patrons come and go,
But never has a thing to say.

Standing there, unable to move,
In this spot, she must stay.
Watching the trucker save a boy
Who almost choked his life away.

Families drifting in and out,
Pass by her as they pay.
No one sees her as they walk by,
Not a nod or "How's your day?"

Stuck here hopelessly in time,
Yearning to leave and play.
Planning an escape is futile
She realizes, to her dismay.

Her time at the diner ends soon.
Today is the last day.
The cook will turn the calendar page.
Tomorrow is the first of May.

CHANGES

Paul checked his pockets one last time. The jingling of his keys gave him false hope that there might be some change left. He doubted it as he looked at the amount of money in his hand. *Maybe it would be enough,* he thought as he put the last of his money on the bar and looked up at the bartender.

"What will this buy me?"

The bartender was a big, hairy man, resembling a brown bear in an apron. He peered over the bar at Paul.

"Don't I know you? Didn't you use to come in here with another guy? Small guy, big mouth?" He looked around the place. "Where is he?"

"Josh?" Paul shook his head. "That guy's not here anymore."

"Oh. Sorry, pal. He was annoying but funny. Made me laugh. Good dancer, too."

"He would have liked hearing that." Paul gestured to the money on the bar. "I'm expecting a few of my friends tonight. We want to celebrate Josh as he was. What will my money buy us?"

The bartender counted out the money and looked back at Paul.

"What do you have in mind? Private room with a few rounds of the house special?"

"Nah, we don't need a private room, just a table off to the side. I'm expecting about ten more guys. Plus, an empty seat for Josh."

"Table for twelve. Got it. You'll get your own waitress and as many pitchers of beer as this cash will cover."

Paul smiled. "Deal! I'm going to wait here until my guests show up."

After the bartender left, Paul looked around the room. His eyes took in the polished brass poles and the deep mahogany of the bar.

How many times had we sat on these stools, Josh? Remember that chick that was too drunk to remember her name?

Paul chuckled to himself as he recalled Josh telling the Barbie clone that maybe one of her tattoos could be a clue to her identity. Josh wouldn't stop teasing her. They had everyone at the bar laughing.

Ah, Josh, your pranks were legendary. When one of our crowd got rattled by your antics, you would slap him on the back and say, 'I'm just Joshin' ya, bro!'

Paul shook his head with laughter until his eyes filled with tears that reminded him that Josh was gone. He let out a deep sigh. He would really miss that guy.

The place was starting to fill up with patrons. Paul took a seat at his reserved table and nodded to his friends as they approached him. The guys exchanged fist pumps and high fives before they got down to serious drinking.

Paul raised his glass to the empty chair on his right. "To you, Josh. We will always remember you as you were."

They all nodded, clinked mugs, gulped down their brews, and turned to the stage.

A stunning brunette had just ascended onto the platform. Caressing the pole before her, she began twirling slowly around it as the music pumped a pulsing beat. She slid around the brass cylinder with a sensuality that Paul had never seen. Her performance was phenomenal! When she finished, Paul's table went wild with hoots, hollers, and applause. They continued their boisterous appreciation of the dancer as she approached their table.

"Hi, guys." Her voice was unusually husky and low.

Paul took her by the hand and stared into her eyes. Everyone at the table watched and waited to see what would happen next.

"We saved you a seat." He gestured to the empty chair. "Can you stay awhile? I have to be honest, we miss you, the old you. But, damn! This new you is incredible!"

She put her hand to her chest and tears filled her eyes. Looking around the table, she said, "Thanks, guys. I appreciate all of you coming here and supporting my decision." She winked at them and continued, "The body may have changed, but, here in my heart, I'm still the crazy prankster you know and love. And I'm not Joshin' you anymore!"

DEVIL IN DISGUISE

Mikey Malarkey and Tony Tortellini were never known for their intelligence. The adventures of these two, however, were notorious throughout the community. Folks still talk, sometimes in hushed voices, about the infamous elevator incident.

It began on a perfect sunny day in April. Mikey and Tony had decided, again, not to attend Roberto Clemente Junior High that day.

As they lolled on Mrs. Tortellini's sofa, they set out a plan to wreak havoc atop the Empire State Building.

"You know, I heard that if you throw a penny off the roof, it could bust a hole through the skull of somebody on the sidewalk," said Tony.

"Nah, that's just an urban legend, dude. But I bet that you could do it with a nickel," countered Mikey.

"Let's take the train to the city and find out, okay? It's too nice to go to school anyway."

Their discussion continued as they jumped the subway turnstile and ran for the number six train headed to Manhattan.

On their way to the famous landmark, the boys lifted some fruit from an outdoor stand and stole sodas from the pretzel vendor. They plotted to drop the fruit from the top of the structure, along with all the coins Tony and Mikey had taken from their mothers' purses.

At the Empire State Building, the youths elbowed their way to the front of the line, making fun of the tourists and families waiting patiently to take the elevator.

When the elevator doors opened, the lads pushed past the disembarking passengers and grinned at each other in evil anticipation.

When they finally arrived at the observation deck, they were so intent on their vile mission, they never even noticed the spectacular view around them. Instead, they searched for a quiet hidden area to launch their dangerous scheme.

"Look at that! Did you see that orange? It just about busted into a bazillion pieces!" Tony said as he looked down to see tiny specks of people hurrying out of harm's way from the citrus grenade.

"Let's try the apple," suggested Mikey as he pushed the hard red fruit through the protective barrier. Both boys watched the explosion of the apple as the startled people below jumped away.

"Now, it's big money time," said Tony.

Together, the boys began hurling various coins through the fence and leaned their faces close to the edge to watch the results. Some pedestrians scurried for cover. People who were not as fast or fortunate were struck with the coins as they looked up in horror. This maneuver rendered painful consequences: an eye was lost, a cheekbone shattered, and a nose broken, all to the delight of Mikey and Tony.

After all their ammunition had been depleted, the dear delinquents headed for the elevator.

Once again, they were oblivious to their surroundings and the fact that the only other person on the deck was a pregnant woman. All three entered the elevator, the mother-to-be staring straight ahead. The two teens watched her, mentally scanning their malevolent repertoire for any mayhem they could garner from this situation.

Suddenly, the elevator lurched to a stop!

The young woman turned to face the boys. Her smile was disingenuous and unnerving. Her eyes were a cold grayish-blue and appeared to be looking right through them. "Well, boys," she said, "We seem to be stuck. We're not going up or down. You know, I can't think of two better travel companions than both of you."

For some unexplained reason, the boys trembled as she took a step towards them.

"We can make the best of this situation, or it could get ugly. Yes, I watched you up there, and I decided to do something about it. Lucky for you, no one was killed, although you did cause serious harm to some innocent bystanders. I mean, how old are you – 13 or 14 years old? That's pretty vicious stuff for such young boys."

She reached out to tousle their hair and they felt both a chill and a searing heat from her touch. They backed up against the wall in fright.

"Tell you what I'm going to do." The woman blew smoke from her fingers as she spoke. "I'm going to do humanity a favor. Something out of character. For me. I'm getting tired of punks like you hurting people and creating victims."

She unbuttoned her jacket and revealed her dark secret, to the terror of Mikey and Tony. The woman was not pregnant! The "bump" was a long, slimy, pointy tail coiled up in front of her. At the moment of her revelation, the elevator began its descent.

She clapped her hands with glee. "Well, well, it looks like we're ready to go. Now, don't you boys worry, you'll fit right in at your new destination. This planet is in enough turmoil and I cannot wait around and let you do more damage. The Big Guy upstairs is getting overrun with innocent victims, and His flock is outnumbering mine. Therefore, my new policy is to be proactive, nip things in the bud, as you may say. So, Mr. Malarkey, Mr. Tortellini, allow me to introduce myself. I'm Belle Z. Bubb, and you two are going down!" She put her arms around both boys and held them tightly.

Back on the observation deck of The Empire State Building, one elevator had been out of commission for almost an hour. It had just stopped running.

When it opened, the operators made a ghastly discovery. Lying on the floor were two heaps of smoldering clothes, accompanied by the stench of burning flesh. It wasn't until the security video was analyzed that the mystery was solved and a new urban legend was born.

DIAMOND GIRL

THUD! The house shook, figurines rattled on the shelf, and Marilyn stood frozen in place, startled by the sound and the quaking walls of her home.

"What the heck was that?" Marilyn worked up enough courage to move and walked around surveying each room for signs of damage.

It wasn't an earthquake. We don't have earthquakes by the shore. Nothing was broken inside the house, better check on things outside.

She opened the door, gasped, and stood motionless, in shock. There, not five feet from her front door, was a huge, gaily wrapped package in the shape of a cube. Marilyn stealthily approached the gigantic box. *Close, but not too close.*

She listened for any sounds that might be emanating from this parcel. Straining her ears, she heard nothing.

Maybe there's a name on it? Marilyn walked around the box, searching for a label of any kind, but found none. *Could it be on the top? I can't see the top. I need a ladder.*

Marilyn climbed the ladder that she propped up against the enormous container. She peered at the top of the package in a futile attempt to find some sort of identification. *If it's at the bottom, I'm out of luck.*

Climbing down from the ladder, she circled the box once more. *Should I open it? I may as well, there might be a clue inside—a tag, a card, something to tell me who this package belongs to.*

She gingerly tore the wrapping paper and examined the box again. She was greeted by a hinged box of royal blue velvet, soft to her touch. *No markings. No labels. No names.*

Now what? Lift the lid? Look inside? Oh, why not? Let's do this! Marilyn ascended the ladder for a second time and struggled with the hinged lid. Grunting and groaning, she finally lifted it up. Looking inside the box, she almost fell off the ladder because of what she saw–the sight took her breath away.

"Whoa!" She steadied herself on the ladder and looked again at the object resting on a bed of white velvet.

It was the biggest diamond ring she had ever seen.

"Where?... What?... Who?"

Her mind was racing with questions. Marilyn looked to the left and right of her house for anyone who would be able to answer her. Then an eerie thought occurred to her. She looked toward the sky.

When Marilyn was a child sitting on the beach, she had a strange idea that God could just thrust His two hands from the clouds and dip them into the ocean to wash them. She half expected to see the hands of the Lord reaching down from the Heavens and using the sea as His own personal washbasin. Her mother blamed the hypnotic motion of the waves for contributing to Marilyn's peculiar scenario.

But now, looking at this ring, Marilyn was certain that there were celestial beings in existence. Here was the proof! A diamond ring that would surely fit God's finger. Well, maybe a goddess because it looked like an engagement ring.

So perhaps her weird ideas weren't so disturbing after all. Could this colossal ring belong to the gods? Had it slipped through the cracks of some divine aperture?

Marilyn came down from the ladder and squinted into the cloudless sky in anticipation of the ring's owner coming to claim it. She saw nothing unusual, but then she heard a rumble in the distance and braced herself for the unknown.

However, the noise did not come from above, but from the road to her left. A large truck slowed down and stopped a few feet from Marilyn and the strange package.

"Afternoon, ma'am," the truck driver said as he exited the cab of his vehicle. "I see you found my cargo. It must have slipped out of the cords I used to fasten it to the bed of my truck."

Marilyn backed away from the box and turned to him. "Tell me, please. What is this for? Is it some kind of…I don't know… some kind of gift for the gods? Is it an offering to the gods?"

The driver laughed. "No, ma'am. It's a prop for a commercial. They're gonna make a video of a girl unwrapping the gift." He looked at the box and chuckled. "I see you got that part done for them."

"That's a very large gift. Must be a really big girl."

"Can't say for sure, ma'am. I'm just the delivery man."

He pushed the box back onto the flatbed, strapped it down, and tested that it was secure.

As he drove away, Marilyn read the logo on the side door of the cab:

Mount Olympus Jewelers
Jewelry Fit for the Gods

END OF THE WORLD

This post-apocalyptic era is really going to suck, thought Vanessa as she cleared the last of the breakfast dishes.

She and her sister, Jane, were still mourning the loss of their father. Actually, Jane, being his favorite, really took it bad. Daddy had died fighting for their freedom.

Freedom to do what? she wondered. *Freedom to keep what's already ours?*

Shaking her head, she walked to Jane's room to look in on her. "Jane, honey? You shouldn't lie down right after you eat. Come out to the living room and keep me company."

Jane turned her back to Vanessa and pulled the blanket over her head, an eerie reminder of all the bodies that had lined the streets in front of their Park Avenue apartment. *So many innocent lives, gone for no good reason.*

The doorbell rang, startling Vanessa.

She patted Jane on her back like a mother burping the baby and whispered, "I'll be right back."

Vanessa cautiously made her way to the door, peering through the peephole. She saw one of the notorious thugs of the neighborhood, Bracco, and two of his goons.

Hah! Bracco—there's a name indicating that even his mother knew he'd never amount to anything. No CEOs named Bracco. No siree, only thugs like this one.

The doorbell rang again.

"Let us in, Vanessa. We know you're in there with that crazy sister of yours."

"What do you want, Bracco?"

"We came for our reward for fighting for your freedom."

Vanessa looked around the apartment. *What reward? Her collection of porcelain cats?*

"If you really fought for my freedom, then I'm free to say go away!"

"Don't force us to break down this door. We want to be thanked properly."

She heard them battering at the heavy door. Apparently, Bracco and his goons were getting too accustomed to having everything their way, preying on the defenseless, old, and sick survivors of the apocalypse.

The thudding continued, louder and more intense. If they kept this up, they were going to destroy the door.

Vanessa took a deep breath and unlocked and opened the door, stepping back as all three of them tumbled in onto the luxuriously carpeted floor.

As they stood up and regained their composure, Bracco moved toward her. "All we want is a little sweet thank you from your sister and you. Not too much to ask, hmmm?"

"Get out of here, you disgusting pig, and take those thugs with you! Even in high school you made me sick. In fact, the whole school thought of you as losers. My father didn't die so your kind could take everything from us."

Bracco angrily reached for Vanessa and she headbutted his face, smashing his nose.

Oh, my God! That hurts, she thought. *Is that equally painful for actors when they do it on TV?*

The maneuver only made Bracco see red through his watering eyes and he charged at her. She kicked him in the crotch. Hard. She smiled as he crumpled to the floor.

The two goons clumsily pulled revolvers out of their pants pockets and pointed them at her with shaky hands.

Vanessa slowly and calmly removed her own weapon tucked behind her in the waistband of her jeans.

Thank you, Lord, for not letting me shoot off my butt cheeks.

"If you do anything stupid, I swear I'll shoot his head right off." She put the gun close to Bracco's left temple.

"Don't listen to her, guys. She ain't got the guts. Silly little goody-goody girl, the high school prom queen. Do it! Kill her! Whaddya waitin' for?"

"Oh, you dumb jerk. You are so clueless about what I can do." In the blink of an eye, Vanessa turned the gun to her left and shot goon number one straight through the heart, causing goon number two to drop his weapon and wet his pants.

Holding her own pistol, she picked up the gun from the floor, pried the other gun out of the dead boy's hands, and turned to Bracco.

"Give it over. Everything you have on you–knives, guns, whatever. Put it all right there." She motioned towards the coffee table with her gun. He put his weapons on the table and backed up.

"Now get up, get out, or get ready for a new war. And take that dead body with you. It was probably your gang that killed our housekeeper, so we no longer have anyone to clean up this mess."

Bracco and his remaining goon carried the bleeding corpse out the door. From the other apartments, heads poked out to watch this scenario.

"You got your reward, my friend. I let you live. Your other reward is that I won't tell anyone how a little goody-goody girl beat you. Nope, I won't spread the word." She looked around at her neighbors and winked at them. "Everyone else is going to do that for me."

When she returned to the apartment, Vanessa was surprised to see Jane scrubbing the floor with soap to remove the blood left by the dead goon.

When did she learn how to clean? And where the hell did she find a bucket and scrub brush?

Jane looked up from the rug and smiled. "I put all those guns on the kitchen counter. Do you think we can get more bullets for them? Daddy taught me to shoot, too, but I was never as good as you."

Vanessa helped her sister remove the rest of the stain.

When they finished, she began making lunch. Jane was up and about, definitely a good sign.

It was midnight when she decided, *Maybe the post-apocalyptic era won't be so bad, after all. My sister and I are tough. We're true survivors.*

Just then, the doorbell rang.

IN THE AIR TONIGHT

In her eyes, they saw no fear;
What made her husband disappear?
The cops were such relentless men,
Who questioned her once and then again.

They asked her if she had a clue
Of this deed, he had planned to do.
Plotting a way to escape this place,
She looked at each inquisitive face.

"Of course I knew, I'm his partner, his wife.
There have been no secrets throughout our life."
Sighing, she told them all one fact.
"He's an illusionist; it's just an act."

"How did he do it? He vanished so well."
Smiling, she said, "Magicians never tell."
"He didn't reappear, the audience saw."
"And he never will." Then she strolled out the door.

I'VE GOT YOU UNDER MY SKIN

"Come in, come in!" The portly man with the lopsided grin held the door ajar for the little dark-haired girl.

"B-but the sign says this place is closed. Where were you? I didn't see anyone when I looked through the display window. "

"Ah, sweet girl, I was expecting you. Or, someone like you." He looked around his shop as she entered. "Now, what can I do for you? Were you looking for something in particular? Please look around. Would you like me to help you with anything?"

She gestured to all the cages, pens, and tanks. "I've never seen creatures like these before. What breeds are they? Are they for sale? If I bought one, how would I take care of it? Do these, um, animals come with care instructions?"

The man took her hand and led her down an aisle crowded with strange living things. "Such a curious child. What's your name, my dear? Allow me to introduce myself to you. I am Gregor Ryan Chant. This is my shop, and these wild beings are … peeves."

"Peeves? You mean like things that bug you? You sell annoying habits and quirks? How profitable can that be? Oh, by the way, I'm Elizabeth, but please call me Lizzie. Now, tell me more about your peeves, please."

"My peeves?' Gregor laughed loudly. "These are not my peeves. These grubby creatures belong to others. People pay me to take away their pet peeves. Just look at those noisy, wooly, shaggy ones in the pen over there. They are Yakkers. They never stop making noise, no matter where they are–an airplane, a bus, a movie theater, even libraries are not safe from the Yakkers."

"Oh, I don't like them. I wouldn't want to be around Yakkers. I like peace and quiet," said Lizzie.

"And here are Ferocious Felinis. They initiate catfights, become very catty, and can never be trusted. When their claws come out, run for shelter, quick. You never know who they will attack next."

"They don't sound nice at all and probably don't make loyal friends. I don't think I want a Ferocious Felini as a BFF. I'd be looking over my shoulder because they don't appear trustworthy at all."

"You're right, and you're a very smart girl, Lizzie. How old are you?"

"I'm eight years old, Mr. Chant. But I've been around long enough to know that you are providing a useful and valuable service to people. Please tell me more about the peeves."

"Well, besides the Yakkers and the Felinis, there are these large, rotund My-Ways."

"My-Ways?"

"Correct. It's short for 'Get Out of My Way'. They push to the fronts of lines, take up handicap parking spots, and simply refuse to follow the rules."

"I've seen them! They are really grabby with a sense of entitlement. Their attitude is 'Me First' which is not a nice attitude to have. What are those slow-moving things in the corner cage?"

"Negative Nellies. Notice they have no tails because they would never wag them anyway. The Negative Nellies are never happy. They see doom and gloom in every room. Steer clear of the Nellies, they are infectious."

Lizzie made a wide path to avoid the Nellies as she and Chant passed the cage.

"Do you have a favorite peeve, Mr. Chant?"

"Me? No, I have no favorites, but I'll tell you about the worst peeves in this place. The ones in this tank. See them?"

"Yes. What's wrong with them? They're just lying around. They seem harmless to me."

"Harmless, you say? Not at all. They are Out and Out Liars. The most treacherous of all peeves. They not only tell lies, but they can't remember the lies that they've told. You'll get a different story every time. Most annoying, frustrating, and disrespectful."

"I agree. Those Out and Out Liars seem to be the most horrible peeves ever."

They stopped walking through the shop. Lizzie noticed the creatures were silently staring at her, telling their stories with their eyes. They didn't start out like this. They were created by people who were insecure, phobic, evil, and mean. Some wanted to change and improve themselves. Others saw nothing wrong in their personalities.

"What about you, Lizzie? Do you have a pet peeve that you'd like to pay me to take from you?"

"Oh no, Mr. Chant. If I got rid of my pet peeves, others would show up to take their place. There's always someone or something getting under your skin, bothering you, or plucking at your last nerve. I'm learning to deal with my little pet peeves."

"Good idea." He clapped his hands together. "Excellent philosophy for such a young lady. Keep those peeves little, and nothing big will ever upset you."

"Goodbye, Mr. Chant," Lizzie said as she headed for the door. "Thank you for letting me tour your establishment. I'll keep my small pet peeves in line."

She walked out onto the sidewalk and turned to wave again to Mr. Chant. The store was gone! A board was nailed diagonally across the dusty glass door. The sign, which was posted on the cracked, dirty window, stated that the building had been condemned and scheduled for demolition the next day.

"Strange," Lizzie whispered to herself. "I wonder where he's taking the peeves. Obviously, someone out there needs his services more than I do."

Lizzie walked down the street, followed by several small yapping, yakking, and hissing furry creatures.

LIGHT MY FIRE

Gather around me, everyone. Are you all sitting comfortably? Good, good. I'm going to try my hand at telling you a scary campfire story. Okay? Listen to this.

We're all familiar with the variations of the teenage couple at the cemetery, one with the escaped hook-handed serial killer, the other ending with a young man hanging from the tree over his own car, and let us not forget the undead, or the ghost of the girl celebrating her birthday.

So I'm going to have to stray from the standard setting and conjure up something new and different.

Let's start with a campground like this one here. Look around, my darlings; it's dark, and there are strange noises to be heard over the crackling of the fire. Hear them? But did you hear anything else? Shhh, listen closely. Sounds like a lost soul is calling for someone.

Do you still hear it? Oh, how sad that voice sounds. Doesn't it break your heart? Almost like a banshee wailing. Wait! Is it getting closer? Why, I believe it is. Scrunch in closer, my sweet campers. Hold hands, link arms; let's not allow this entity to break our bond. I see all your eyes wide with fear, but there is nothing to worry about as long as we are united in our goal to stay safe.

No, no, don't panic, even though it seems that the noise is coming nearer. It's not as sad as it sounds it before? Don't you think it appears angrier? I can't imagine why the tone changed like that. Perhaps we should huddle even closer. The fire is warm and chases away the dark. So let's stay here just a while longer. Okay?

No sense trying to get back to the security of our cabin. Whatever we are hearing is now between us and the trail leading back to our shelter. Fear not, my darlings, together we will be strong. I promise you all, we will get through this tonight. By morning, this horrible noise will be just a memory. You don't believe me? You think I made this up to scare you all? Now, my children, you look cynical and doubtful. We are out here alone, well, with one uninvited guest pining away. Who would I get to play such a terrible trick on you? I do not know anyone that mean. Out here, we love children. We love you all very much. Very, very much.

So my little chickens and dumplings, just sit still, continue to hold on to each other. Oh, by the way, will some of you hold these carrots? Can't you hear me over that screeching? I said, "Hold these carrots." You there, can you put some of these sliced potatoes in your pockets? I'm not sure if it will ward off the impending doom facing us, but it couldn't hurt.

Oh, my lovely little ducklings and dear lambs, don't be scared. Everyone, squeeze your eyes shut, real tight. Tighter! Do not open them until I say so. Now… just… let… me …get …up…and …move this… umph… large cauldron that has been slowly sliding down the rocky path towards us.

Perhaps you'll all feel safer if you just climb in. Say, what now? It's filled with water? That's to keep away the evil entity, honest. Are all of you inside? Great!

Now let me push this over the fire… just to keep you warm, of course.

JANIE'S GOT A GUN

Janie rested her head against the window of the bus while she shifted uncomfortably in her seat. The glass pane felt cool on her forehead. As the vibration of the vehicle droned through her brain, she tried to block out the noises from the passengers around her. Meaningless conversations sounded like the buzzing of bees or the constant hum of a refrigerator. Dull dialogues like "Did you see last night's game? What a phenomenal pass!"

"Yeah, that was a beautiful move. Cost me a fortune with my bookie. When it comes to betting on the game, from now on, I'll make my own pass."

Janie had heard lines like that too often. They were burned into her head, like the scars burned onto her arms from the cigars her stepfather smoked and extinguished on her. For years, she and her family had been his punching bags and targets for his animosity.

But now, she had to concentrate on herself, her future, and her safety. Janie caught herself fiddling with the clasp of her purse. She drew in her breath and stopped. *Oh no! What if my purse had opened? What if the other people on the bus saw what I was carrying?* She looked around furtively and clutched the leather satchel closer to her body.

Be calm, stupid. No one here can read your mind. They have no clue who you are, what you did, or where you are headed.

A woman on a cell phone said, "There's nothing anyone can do now. It's over, done with. I'm leaving town tonight."

Janie craned her neck to get a glimpse of the woman as she spoke on her cell in hushed tones.

Is she talking about me? How does she know I'm leaving town? Was she watching me today? Did she follow me here?

Now, Janie was getting nervous. She played the woman's conversation over and over in her mind. "There's nothing anyone can do now."

There definitely was nothing anyone could do now. Not that anyone did anything to help me when I was pleading for comfort, shelter, and safety.

"It's over, done with." *That's right. It was finally over.* Her stepfather was no longer going to hurt her or any other family member. Janie had taken matters into her own hands and solved her problem without anyone's help.

"I'm leaving town tonight." *Yes, yes, I am.* She had her fake I.D. and the sweet little .22 revolver she had bought from the gang member who hung around her high school. He assured her that the piece could never be traced, and she promised herself that she would never leave home without it. She was going to start over–new hair color, a new beginning, and a determination to rise above the torment she endured from childhood. She was giving herself a clean slate. No more monster stepfathers, no more sleepless nights, and no tears left in her.

The bus slowed to a stop. The driver turned to the passengers and announced that there appeared to be some kind of roadblock ahead.

Janie panicked! She took deep breaths and covered her purse with her sweater. She looked out the window, feigning nonchalance as the bus eased closer and closer to the flashing blue lights.

The doors of the bus opened and two state troopers entered. They looked ominous with their wide-brimmed hats and crew cuts. Janie pretended to be examining her chewed cuticles as the troopers conversed with the driver. The words *"Don't move. Don't look around. Play it cool."* seemed to echo through her skull.

These guys are huge and scary! What do they want? Do they know about me?

The broad-shouldered men were bending their heads as they cautiously walked down the aisle of the bus, looking at the faces of each passenger.

What is that in their hands? Are they holding a photograph? Is it a picture of me?

Feeling faint, Janie closed her eyes and sunk further into her seat.

"Miss, can you come with us, please?"

Janie opened her eyes and saw the state troopers looming over the woman who had been talking on her cell phone.

Janie looked skyward as the troopers escorted the strange woman off the bus. "Thank you, God. I'm taking this as a sign. It's only You and me from now on. And things are never gonna be the same."

JUST BREATHE

Beth was startled awake by the sound of the alarm and the announcements: "Good morning, Young Patriots. Please note the time now is 6 AM. Nutrition will be served in the main dining room starting at 6:30 AM and ending at 7:30 AM. Virtual classes will begin promptly at 7:45 AM. Please be ready to sign on."

Beth rose from her bed, went to her wardrobe and removed one of her eight jumpsuits. They were all the same, a muted mustard color to denote that she was a teenager.

At fourteen, Beth was supposed to have started high school, but that didn't happen. Nothing good or celebratory had happened. The only thing that did occur was this Disease. The Disease changed everyone's life except for the Elite. They just managed to get richer, happier, and more powerful.

Beth also lost her grandparents at the beginning of the Disease. It seemed that since the elderly were just "sucking up money" from the pockets of the Elite, they were exposed to the Disease to "test the strength of the strain." Seventy-five percent of those seniors perished within the first three months, saving the Elite any probable financial stress.

She was also part of a group of parentless children, PeeCees, for short.

Her mother lost her store when small businesses were ordered to close their doors due to the Disease. Scrambling and struggling to pay their bills depleted their savings, and her mother decided that if she committed suicide, her daughter could live off the insurance money. But that didn't happen, either. No money was given to Beth. She was informed that all funds were part of the Coalition, where no-one carried money, no-one owned homes, and nothing belonged to just one person.

Except for the Elite. They owned everything and doled everything out.

You received your food and services by the number of hours you put in. As children, your worth was based on your grades, how you listened, and how you responded to the virtual lecturers. The more points you got for good behavior, the more they accumulated in your service bank.

For the good of the citizens, there were no more law enforcement officers. They were not needed anymore, due to the installment of Peacekeepers. Police officers and their families were invited to leave the area immediately. They took up that suggestion and moved out of the state.

That wasn't all. Freethinkers were never heard from again. Beth had no idea where they could be or what happened to them.

A wall was built around the area and it was called NOW, a New Ordered World. And the New Ordered World did not welcome intruders.

The New Ordered World did not want its citizens to know about anything going on beyond those walls. It wasn't necessary. The New Ordered World took care of you. The Peacekeepers made sure there were no free or critical thinkers within the boundaries of the wall. You did what you were told, were expected to accept everything as truth, and no more was to be said about it.

Beth felt alone as she passed her childhood friends in the halls when they went to Nutrition. They could only look at each other over the masks which covered their mouths. They could not even smile at each other. Nor could they form silent words since they were always being watched. Beth knew there was even a camera in her cubicle–also known as her room. It contained a bed, a wardrobe, and a desk with a laptop. The color of her walls was mustard, like her jumpsuit.

Smaller children wore jumpsuits of a muted olive green hue. As you moved up in age or were assigned an occupation, the color of your jumpsuit would change.

When you were 13, the Coalition provided you with the mustard color; at 18, you were given a gray jumpsuit.

During your 18th year, you took various physical, mental, and academic tests to determine the occupation permanently assigned to you. The color of your jumpsuit would match that occupation. There were no pinks or blues, as gender was no longer recognized. There were no black or white jumpsuits, either. There were no bright colors, and only the Elite wore gold or silver. Many of the Elite wore pants suits in the style of the 70s.

Beth knew things like that because she used to be a history buff. Even as a little girl, Beth had total recall of everything she read and learned.

Beth suspected this New Ordered World was wrong. Everyone was no longer free. They were not anything but pawns of the Elite. Citizens were assembling items, manufacturing things, doing stuff by hand to please the Elite. They sold everything that was being made to the outsiders for their own gain. All you received was nutrition and a place to sleep.

There were no longer churches, no social gatherings, no movie theatres, and no malls. Why open a mall if there was nothing to buy? You had your jumpsuits, no need for pretty clothes since social gatherings were banned. Even television only provided shows that were approved by the Elite and the Peacekeepers.

The Peacekeepers made sure you stayed where you belonged, that you did not mingle, that you did not interact. "It's not healthy. You could die! You could contract the Disease. You could bring it to others!!!"

What others? Beth thought. *Who am I seeing? Who am I interacting with? My virtual learning is only regurgitating what you're telling me and what you're telling me is wrong.*

What I'm learning is wrong. All I'm learning is that anything outside these walls is evil and that an evil man once ruled us, but now the New Ordered World would take care of us and protect us from the EVIL. But I believe this evil is worse. We have nothing, morale is low, and many people are trying to kill themselves. Even at the nutrition tables, you're not given anything that could be dangerous. Everyone is silent. You can only pull down your mask to eat, and if you are caught looking at or gesturing to anyone else, you will be taken away by the Peacekeepers.

Beth didn't know if you were punished or dismissed– that's what she called it when you were sent away and never seen again. Were you put outside the walls? She thought that would probably be a reward. She worried about the Peacekeepers because she recalled that they were once regular people. Now they were trained by and worked with the Elite. The community was a disaster inside the walls. Everything was spray-painted, cars had been burned, buildings defaced with drawings of freethinkers hanging from nooses, cemetery headstones knocked over, and select statues removed. The Elite allowed this because, with no more history, everybody should be happy and harmoniously concentrate on the present.

Beth spent every day looking for something to use that would end her miserable unfortunate 14-year-old life. She couldn't go on this way.

She remembered it had all started on Friday the 13th, the night she was supposed to go to the Lucky Stars dance. Her long time crush had asked her. Oh, how excited she had been! Beth had a new dress, and her mother was going to let her wear lipstick for the very first time! It was going to be glorious. Her grandparents would be working in the store, so her mother could make sure that Beth's hair was perfect. Beth had tingled with excitement when she practiced applying lipstick.

She wished to turn time back to that day again. She wanted to see her grandparents, to be held and hugged by them. Beth yearned to talk with her mother, and tell her how much she was loved.

There wasn't even a funeral for her mother. You were only allowed to view the body through a window. Then they just took her body away. Beth didn't even know where it went. She had nothing, absolutely nothing. So did lots of other children, they had no parents. Parents were mandated to surrender their children, but the children were told their parents abandoned them. Children could be manipulated and intimidated and made to fear the consequences if they did not follow directions and the rules. The Peacekeepers walking around with their automatic weapons lent more to the threats than anything else.

After her lessons, Beth submitted her homework, signed off, and laid back down on her bed. She could watch TV if she wanted to, but it was always the same shows. The same news was repeatedly broadcasted all the time: "Everything outside the walls is devastatingly evil. Everything inside these walls is good." In her head, Beth prayed for some kind of peace. If she were ever caught praying…well…she shuddered to think what would happen.

She could read any of the approved literature, if she wanted. There was no library per se–you had to ask for reading material by typing the title into the little laptop attached to her desk. Everything seemed to be chained down, including the allotted toiletries.

She put her arms over her eyes as she lay back on her pillow.

Beth must've drifted off to sleep, a sleep she welcomed but wished would last forever.

* * *

She woke up to the annoying sound of the alarm. "Wake up, darling, it's time to get up."

Beth stretched her arms, opened her eyes, looked around, and blinked. She was her in her old room! Her blue bedroom decorated with pictures of the ocean and seashells. The dress for the dance was hanging up on her closet door. *Is this possible? Is this really her mom, alive and well, gently shaking her?*

"I thought you were too excited about the dance to sleep, but I'm glad that you slept after all." Beth's mother looked away for a second, then turned back with a wavering smile. "I'm afraid that I have some distressing news. It seems we are now in the middle of a pandemic. The Lucky Stars dance was canceled. I just got the news. In fact, all classes have been canceled until further notice. I also got word that I can't run my business right now. I have to go there now, shut it down, and lock it up.

"You're going to be on your own today, my dear, because your grandparents don't feel so well. I hope there's nothing seriously wrong with them. They're so sweet but so fragile." Her mother let out a sigh. "I'm sorry, Beth. I don't know when this nightmare will end but bear with me. We will get through this together, you and I."

Beth's eyes welled up with tears as she held her mother's hands. She said, "No, Mom, no. We will not get through this together. We will not get through this at all. This nightmare is just beginning." She lay her head back down on the pillow and sobbed uncontrollably.

Her mother whispered, "I promise, cross my heart, and hope to die."

LIFE IN THE FAST LANE

Jenny watched the spider as it crawled across her windshield. She stared past the arachnid to the line of traffic blocking the entrance to the turnpike.

Why, oh, why are we not moving? This spider could create two webs in the time it takes this jam to clear.

Looking over to the other lane, she saw the cars traveling past the tollbooth in a steady stream. Jenny watched the grey SUV with the dinosaur decal in that other lane. Once, it had been in front of her; now, it was already leaving her line of vision. Sighing, Jenny thought, *Just my luck. I always pick the wrong lane, the wrong line, and definitely the wrong life.*

With that thought, something clicked inside Jenny's brain. *What made that particular lane of cars move faster than hers? Why didn't she choose that lane when she had the chance?*

Jenny shook her head. *And why hadn't she waited for Mr. Right instead of giving in to pressure to marry the most popular guy in high school all those years ago?* Like her car, mired in this log jam of vehicles, she was stuck in this nowhere marriage.

Would life in the fast lane be any better? she wondered as she glanced again at the moving cars in the next path. *Most likely, they're happier than I am right now. Will they reach their goals way before me because all these obstacles don't hinder them? We're all heading in the same direction, just like in the real world. We all want the same things for ourselves and our families. But how are we getting there, and at what speed?*

Finally, the cars in front of her began moving forward. Jenny was elated. She would reach her destination. Maybe not at the time she had planned, still, she would get there. As she drove, the radio station played her favorite songs, making the trip more pleasant. It was as if her little red sports car was apologizing for steering her into the wrong situation.

Jenny patted the dashboard. "Not to worry, baby. We're doing fine. Just a little setback. You know I can overcome any hurdle, especially now." This last line was directed more to herself than her car.

From the corner of her eye, Jenny noticed that the automobiles on her left were slowing down, almost to a complete halt. Consequently, the cars in her own lane were reducing speed, going into what she called the 'Duh-Lookee-Dere' pace.

"Well, well, it seems that the grass is not greener in the passing lane," Jenny muttered to herself. "Maybe I was right in taking the slower lane, being patient, and putting up with a little inconvenience. My reward is to keep moving forward and leave that bad scene behind." She gave her car one last pat. "I am still talking about this journey and not my sad little life, right?"

With not much further to go, Jenny stole a look at the cause of the delay. It was the grey SUV with the dinosaur decal! The truck was on its side, the front crushed, and all the windows shattered. No other vehicle appeared to be involved.

Wow! What could have happened there? A blowout? Mechanical error? Too much to drink? Her lips curved up in a small smile. *Or maybe the driver unknowingly drank something poisonous…*

She pondered the issue some more. *Should I have stopped? Were there enough emergency vehicles on the way? What shall I do now?*

Jenny lowered the radio and whispered, "Just keep going. You're almost there, don't look back." She thought about the spider that had crossed her path earlier on her ride and hoped it was okay somewhere.

Because some living things deserve to keep on going unharmed, but other life forms, the evil ones, the mean kind, the hurtful sort, they call for the need to be punished.

It was a promise she silently made to herself as she and hubby drank to their separate vacations. He was going "hunting" a euphemism for seeing his mistress. Jenny was going to a retreat to heal her broken arm, black eye, and bruised ribs.

She had raised her drink, pretending this last beating was a distant memory and nothing was wrong. Yes, as their glasses clinked, she waited for her husband, Terrance, to finish his vodka and lime.

Terrance, T-Rex to his friends, belched and smacked her butt as he said, "See ya in a few weeks, bitch."

Jenny winked at him as he packed his grey SUV–the one with the T-Rex decal–and drove away.

Then she started for her car–not just to follow him, but to begin her journey as a very merry widow.

NO TIME LEFT FOR YOU

The man who approached Victoria seemed so familiar, she smiled and boldly took his hand. His countenance radiated with happiness.

"Welcome, my dear. I hope you weren't waiting too long."

"No, not at all. At least I don't think so. Do I know you? I feel like I've seen you before, but I can't recall your name, Mr. uh—."

"Call me Peter. No need for formalities here." He pointed to a large, white over-stuffed sofa. "Please have a seat and let's chat."

Victoria felt her essence sink comfortably down as she sat. It was as if fluffy, loving arms were embracing her. In front of her was a huge video screen covering the entire wall. Her curiosity was piqued. Peter produced a golden clipboard from under his robe and settled in next to her.

"I must ask you a few questions before we proceed any further." He held a silver quill in his hand and continued. "How old are you?"

Victoria stared at her hands, once veined and gnarled, but now smooth and surprisingly youthful-looking. "I believe I'm—I was 94 years old."

"What's the last thing you can remember?"

"Falling. I think it was a dream. I was plummeting, actually. Not sure what happened after that." She gasped. "Could it have been that dream where, once you hit the ground, you're really dead?"

"You weren't dreaming, you were skydiving. While taking in the sights and enjoying your flight, you delayed in pulling the cord."

"Oh. Am I a little puddle of flesh and bones somewhere?"

"No, you're hanging from a tree. Your body has been found because the spectators watched you closely, and the crowd dashed to your landing point."

Victoria sat pensively, taking in all he had said, trying to recall her last breathing moment. It was futile. Her mind was blank.

"Is there anything in your life that you regret not doing? That you left unfinished or never fulfilled? In other words, did you have a bucket list?"

"Hmm…there was one thing I always wanted to do. It was the first item on my bucket list…I wanted to juggle."

Peter looked up at her. "That's it? In your 94 years on earth, you regret not becoming a juggler?'

"It's not for lack of trying. When I was in grade school, I thought it would be fun to amuse my classmates by juggling."

"But you told them jokes, made up funny stories, and helped them with their classwork instead."

"During my high school years, it would've been a great talent to have. Juggling commands attention."

"Weren't you taking college courses in addition to your regular classes? Plus, you were involved in chorus, sports, dance, and the school paper." Peter was writing furiously as he spoke. "You also had the constant presence of your childhood sweetheart. Your calendar was extremely full."

Victoria sighed. "While in college, I wanted so much to be able to take three oranges from the cafeteria and just start tossing them in the air. How cool would that have been?"

"Ah, college! Yes, you overloaded your program so that you could graduate early. Don't forget your part-time job and planning your wedding. Keeping that busy would have prevented anyone from having a free moment."

"Then I had my family to raise, my career as an educator, president of several community organizations, involvement in my children's sports, and my own private tutoring business."

"Not to mention caring for your ailing grandmother, followed by the demands of your mother's poor health. Too many events to balance."

"Still, as a science teacher, I thought it would have been so admirable to juggle a few planets for the class."

Victoria turned to watch her life video that had been playing on the giant screen. "In my twilight years, my hands were too shaky even to keep my tea from splashing; never mind flinging anything in the air!" She shrugged. "So I never learned to juggle. A rather simple aspiration that I failed to accomplish."

Peter laughed. "Oh, my dear, you couldn't be any more mistaken." He put down the clipboard and took her hands in his. "You've had a lucrative career, a wonderful family, friends who always counted on you, and a satisfying life. You juggled more things than many circus performers I've seen, and I have seen them all!" He smiled and went on, "I can offer you a choice which is not common here. Do you wish to stay here, or would you prefer to return to earth and fulfill your desire to be a juggler?"

It took a while for Victoria to make her decision. She weighed the pros and cons of the situation–staying in paradise as a reward for her long and happy life versus returning to earth as a new tiny human starting over. Blissful eternity or total uncertainty?

She turned to Peter and clasped her hands. "I've made my decision!"

* * *

Far below the heavens, a young mother held her newborn baby girl and looked up at her husband. "Renaldo," she whispered, "Isn't she beautiful? What should we name her? Do you think she'll enjoy being part of the circus? Look at her hands. I can picture them juggling at a very young age. Don't you agree?"

Renaldo bent down to view his daughter. "Yes, Maria, our child is a beauty. Yet, I would rather she not be part of our three-ring circus. She should go to college, do something different, and be someone other than a performer." He looked off towards the door of their trailer as if he were envisioning the future. "Yes, college! She can have any career she chooses. It will be a victory for our family. In fact, we'll name her Victoria, the girl who will not juggle."

At those words, the baby girl would not stop crying.

ONE THING LEADS TO ANOTHER

Walter finished the last cream-filled doughnut as he struggled to get out of his recliner. This maneuver only confirmed the belief that he had grown massive these past ten weeks while in "quarantine." Remaining in place, working from home meant no long walks from the train to his office. Even the gym was closed. Local leaders advised everyone to "stay home, save lives." Walter heeded these directives while easing his frustration with carbs, sugars, and fats.

During his morning channel surfing exercises, in which he had achieved Olympic medal status, he happened upon an 'As Seen on TV' advertisement for the 'guaranteed to lose weight, trendsetting, state-of-the-art 91Divoc Drone-Nanny!'

Walter perked up as he wrote down the 1-800 number and website address for this product. The commercial continued, "The Drone-Nanny was created to monitor your food intake and exercise regimen and apply behavior modification strategies. Order within the next 60 minutes, and receive free shipping. That's right! Get your Drone-Nanny within 48 hours of purchase. Time is running out!"

A small clock in the lower-left corner of the screen ticked off the 60-minute countdown. Walter was giddy as he bought the Drone-Nanny online.

Imagine! Guaranteed weight loss and a motivation to exercise. He couldn't wait to get it. After confirming his purchase, he hoisted his bulk out of the chair in search of potato chips.

The day the Drone-Nanny arrived, Walter practically tore the box apart in gleeful anticipation. He gently lifted the baseball-size sphere out of the package as if it were a

Faberge egg. Ready to begin his adventure, he lovingly held the drone as he read the instructions:

1. Activate the drone by pressing the button on top.
2. Point the drone's "eye" at your face to take a photo for facial recognition.
3. Speak into the drone's microphone by
   a) saying your full name
   b) slowly recite the alphabet starting with A and ending with Z
   c) say this sentence clearly - The quick brown fox jumps over the lazy dog.
4. Now you are ready to enjoy the care that Drone-Nanny provides.
5. God bless and Godspeed.

God bless and Godspeed? That must be some sort of joke.

Walter followed the directions and watched as the lighted globe hovered before him. He tested its tracking potential by shifting himself in his chair. As he moved to the right, the drone moved with him.

This is so freaking cool! Walter was pleased.

Later that day, Walter got up to look for the chocolate bunnies, bought for the Easter that never was. The drone followed him as if it were helping him with his search. As he reached for the sweet brown rabbits, a short quick electric shock hit his back

"Ouch! What the hell—?" The drone had tased him! Walter kept his eye on the floating ball and reached for an apple. The drone continued to hover silently. He closed his hand around the chocolate bunny again and ZAP! The pain shot through his back once more.

Oh, no! No, no, no. This is not good. Effective, yes, but painful. Walter decided to give this type of weight loss strategy a week. He was interested in who would win this war of the wills.

* * *

Day seven found Walter hiding in his closet as the drone kept banging against the tightly-shut door. It knew Walter was sitting on the floor eating those chocolate bunnies. He had cleverly snuck in the sweets by blocking the drone's view and hiding them in his laundry basket. Walter congratulated himself on his ingenuity and licked the chocolate off his fingers. Smacking his lips, he opened the closet door, carrying some sweaters in his arms, which he hoped would throw the drone off track.

ZZZZZZAPPPPZZZZTH!

Not only was this shock longer, but the pain was also more intense. Walter ran through the house, trying to lose the evil sphere following him. Then the drone slowed down and stopped tasing him. This inactivity puzzled Walter. He stopped to catch his breath and pondered the situation. Of course! He was exercising. No tasing for that. But, because he had stopped, the drone moved closer. Walter held up his hands in surrender and jogged in place.

He moved over to the instruction booklet and looked for a way to turn off the drone. Nothing. He then looked for a return address. *Damn. There's no name and no place to send it back.* He searched for the website. It no longer existed. And the 1-800 number had been disconnected! His eye caught the "God bless and Godspeed" on the instruction booklet. *Well I now know what that means.*

Walter collapsed in his chair from exhaustion and stress. *What am I going to do? What can I do?* Gradually a plan formed in his mind. He stared at the devilish drone and smiled.

* * *

Walter spent another tedious week of submitting to the drone, but it was worth it. He was now twelve pounds lighter and decidedly healthier. However, Walter was still a prisoner in his own home, not just due to the pandemic, but also to the ghoulish globe.

Seven days ago, Walter had ordered reflective material, similar to aluminum foil, and he crafted a hazmat suit of the fabric, complete with head covering. While wearing this attire, Walter would reach for cookies, candies, cake, ice cream, or anything fattening, and the sinister sphere would send out its electronic impulses, each more intense than the last.

ZAP ZAP PFFT! ZAP ZAP PFFT!

But, because of the mirrored hazmat suit he wore, the shock path darted back to the drone. Little by little, the metal skin of the drone became worn away. Walter taunted the drone and snickered each time it tased itself.

Finally, it spun wildly, and with a pop and a fizzle, the drone burst into pieces, which fell to the floor.

Walter yelled, "WHOOP!" and jumped for joy. It was gone! The bully of a ball was no more! He was free! OK, free of the drone, but still restricted by the health department. Yet, the feeling of relief and reprieve was like no other sensation he had ever experienced. Walter cleaned up the melted, shiny mess, put it in a plastic bag, tied it tight, and walked outside to toss the remains of his nightmare into the communal garbage bin.

As Walter neared the bin, the beautiful sunny day turned dark and shadowy. He looked up, eyes wide and mouth open to scream. To his horror, another drone, fifty times larger than the one he had destroyed, was hovering over him and his house. The label on the side read 91Divoc Drone-Big Daddy. He turned to run.

Walter was entirely incinerated before he could reach his front door.

PEACE TRAIN

"Come on, we're gonna be late!" Pulling her along the platform of the train station, I could tell that Miranda (Randy for short) was still hesitant about this trip. But I had persuaded her and guaranteed that it would be fun. "After all, YOLO–you only live once!" I had reminded her.

"A Murder Mystery Train ride where the guests become part of the mystery? You can't refuse, Randy-girl."

"I don't like these things. They force me to act and put me on the spot."

"Don't be silly. How can it be a bad thing? If you're not totally blown away by this trip, I promise next time we'll do whatever safe and sound activity you like. I'll even give you back your ticket money."

"But it's a two-day trip. That's a lot of time to spend on a train just for a show."

"And what did you have planned for that time? I can tell you–nothing. Not a thing. Come on, girlfriend. We'll have a terrific time, I swear."

As we ran across the platform, I shouted to Randy one more time. "Come on, hurry! I don't want to miss it."

Fortunately, we made it to the train with enough time to check our bags. The outside of the train was painted black and looked foreboding.

It must be part of the show, I figured. The writing along each car was gothic and read DEATH TRAIN. *Well, there's no mystery there, huh?*

As we entered the reception car, we were greeted by an elderly man in a tuxedo who offered us drinks from a silver tray. Neither one of us took a glass. We had our own water bottles, and it was too early in the day to imbibe.

"What's in the glass, anyway?" I asked the disappointed waiter.

"It's the Death Train's signature drink. I do wish you'd have some–to toast your journey."

"Nah, we'll wait for the show tonight before we start drinking."

"Show?" He seemed confused. "Yes, of course, the show tonight. By the way, the dining car will be serving dinner in one hour."

Too excited to be hungry, we went to the club car to relax and mingle with our fellow travelers. As we watched the scenery glide by the window, dozens of passengers, actors and non-actors, I guess, also settled in the car. The conversation built up to a blaring pitch.

But our attention was pulled to a couple, three tables away from us. They were coughing loudly enough to be heard over the din of the conversations.

The realization hit me. They weren't coughing; they were choking, gagging, and frothing at the mouth.

Randy and I were the only ones watching them as everyone else went about their business.

What kind of murder mystery this, with no reaction to those two people? Shouldn't we at least feign surprise or pretend to help?

As the couple finally stopped writhing and slumped over the table, our colleagues raised their own glasses to toast their departure. This bizarre act was followed by another group of passengers, at the other end of the car, coughing and choking.

I looked at Randy in disbelief. "What the hell is going on?" I muttered under my breath.

We nonchalantly got up from our booth, each holding a glass, making it appear as if we were drinking, too, and exited the car. Still, this maneuver did not guarantee our safety. Walking through the next car, we observed several passengers slouched over the burgundy seats. Some seemed to be sleeping, but we knew better.

"Let's find our cabin," I whispered. "We need to speak in private."

Randy and I struggled to look unphased as we edged our way to the sleeping cars.

There was an eerie silence inside the train, accompanied by the hypnotic sound of metal on metal outside. It sounded like "Can't turn back. Can't turn back. Can't turn back."

I don't know what was happening, but I certainly knew I was not paranoid. Something was wrong, very wrong.

In the privacy of our small cabin, Randy and I discussed what we thought was transpiring. This was not a murder mystery train ride at all. This was a suicide convoy streaking to hell.

"We have to get off," I said.

"How? Are we going to jump?"

"No, I'll pull the emergency cord. The train has to stop. Then we'll slip out between the cars and jump. It's our only way to escape. Look, I'll do it now. We're about to approach a stockyard. We can get help there."

Outside our cabin, we inched as close to the end of the car as possible. Then I pulled the cord nearest the door. The shrieking sound of the train braking scraped through our ears as the car slowed down.

We opened the door and came face-to-face with the elderly waiter, still carrying his tray.

"You can't leave! You have to stay until you reach your final destination."

"That's what you think, old man– get out of our way!" I pushed him aside and leaped off the train step and into the brush surrounding the tracks.

Randy was about to jump when the old man grabbed her. Suddenly, he looked taller; his tuxedo had turned into a black hooded robe, and the tray became a scythe.

Randy screamed as he enveloped her, and the train started back up and picked up speed again.

It disappeared from my sight and I have a feeling that it's never coming back… and neither is Randy.

RUNNING WITH THE DEVIL

The gunshot broke the silence and made Katie gasp. Her mind raced as she tried to regulate her breath.

Come on, girl, if you start breathing too hard, everything will be over. Concentrate. Take small, even breaths. You're a fighter, a winner.

Katie attempted to stay centered by running through her head the events that led to this day. She stared straight ahead, not looking around for fear that any distraction could possibly make her breathe harder and faster. *Take it easy. You can do this. Stay on target.* Her chest was beginning to hurt, as was her left side. Katie, still striving to control her breathing, thought about all the good things in her life. She was getting tired, but the pain in her chest was spreading and screaming at her not to give up. She couldn't hear anyone nearby and still refused to turn her head to see if she was really alone. Katie mentally encouraged herself to stay alert in spite of the excruciating throbbing throughout her body.

Her breath was coming faster, pounding in her ears, drowning out her own thoughts. If there were any other sounds around her, she couldn't hear them anyway. She was sweating, feeling clammy. It was so very dark. It had been dark for a very long time.

* * *

Katie squinted her eyes. There it was! Just like they said it would be–the lights at the end of the tunnel. She hoped to see her family at the other end. The idea of being with her loved ones sent her hurtling towards the light. As she got closer to the brilliance, Katie heard music: lilting, upbeat, and beautiful. *It's okay, girl, go for it. You're almost there. It will be over soon.* The light was her goal now, and she was happy to be heading there.

Katie gulped for air as she broke the ribbon stretched across the tunnel. She collapsed into the arms of a reporter closest to the finish line.

"Katie Harrigan, you have come in first place in the St. Patrick's Day Shamrock Tunnel run. You finally beat your rival! Congratulations!"

Catching her breath, Katie smiled at the reporter and searched for her family. She saw them waiting at the refreshment stand. She thanked the reporter and then heard him say, "Here's your competitor now. Patty O'Mara just came in second, and she does not look happy. No, not in the least bit happy."

Katie shrugged and headed towards her parents. Unlike the starter gun heard at the beginning of the race, the loud band music concealed the sound of these gunshots. Katie didn't hear them. She only felt the intense pain in her chest. Then she felt nothing. Nothing at all.

SLEEP LIKE A BABY TONIGHT

It wasn't the first time I had seen a fight like this. However, each one gets better than the last, and this last one was the best.

As I sat in the back of Mama Bernadette's Rest Stop, I observed a sad-looking family enter the restaurant. The man was dressed in a heavy down jacket, leather gloves, and a fur hat with flaps. Yet, he had a scowl on his face, like the world and everything in it had angered him since birth.

The woman was pale, so pale that her bruises stood out on her face and arms like neon lights. She had on a short-sleeved sweater dress that appeared to be unraveling.

The children, a boy and a girl, were skittish and looked ready to cower at the least little sound. The boy was about seven years old and wearing a T-shirt faded to the point where the logo could no longer be read. His jeans were hanging off his bony frame, and his sneakers were shredded. The girl was a little older, maybe nine years old, and wore a frayed sundress with a thin sweater covering her skinny arms. She had on dirty canvas sneakers with no socks.

When I saw them, I felt the February chill go through me, even though I was clad in a thick woolen sweater and fleece-lined boots over my jeans. No longer interested in the book I was reading or the coffee (Bernadette's Brew) I was nursing, I gave my full attention to this gloomy group as they sat down. They definitely intrigued me.

"Welcome to Mama Bernadette's. Can I get you a drink while you look at the menu?" The waitress handed out laminated placemats, which listed all the delectable items offered by Mama Bernadette.

"I want a beer, straight from the tap. None of that canned crap for me. Ya got that, Toots?" His voice was so loud I believe we all got his order.

"Okay, sir. What about you, ma'am? And you guys? I bet you all could use a nice hot cocoa, right?"

"They don't want nothin'. I'm the one who's been drivin' all night with these three. I did all the work; I get the prize–a burger and a beer. Maybe even two beers for me."

The children looked down at their placemats in silence. You could tell they were hungry, thirsty, and cold. My heart was breaking.

"Can we just have water, please?" The woman was asking the man as if she needed his permission.

All eyes of the restaurant patrons were now on him. I'm sure he felt their stares boring into his head.

"Yeah, sure. You must've worked up a real thirst gettin' us lost and findin' this hole-in-the-wall here. Bring these geniuses some water." One could feel the soundless sigh that was in each patron's mind. At least they would have water.

The waitress returned shortly with a huge hamburger and a large mug of beer.

She also placed a cup of cocoa and a small sandwich in front of each child and the woman.

"What's this? Get it outta here! I didn't order no food for them."

"It's on the house, compliments of Mama Bernadette. There's no charge, sir."

Just as he was about to sweep everything off the table in a rage, a meaty and muscular hand landed on his shoulder. "I wouldn't do that…pal. Mama Bernadette don't like people tossin' good food onto the floor."

The man looked up to see a guy the size of a small grizzly bear looming over him.

"Now, we don't want no trouble here, so why not let your little family enjoy their meal?"

The man noticed the people around the room, mostly women, who were sitting and watching him with contempt. He was becoming a little wary and slightly suspicious. This was no ordinary restaurant. He was finally catching on.

Turning to his wife, he sputtered, "You! You brought me here on purpose! We aren't lost. You KNEW where we were going." He reached over the table to strike her. It was the last thing he did–or tried to do.

All of us rose from our chairs carrying our weapons of choice: pool cues, empty beer bottles, and cast iron cooking utensils. We had been waiting for this moment.

"You shoulda kept your hands to yourself."

'Mama Bernadette' put both his big hands on the man's shoulders, pushing him down further into the chair.

The woman scooted away from the table to a safe corner of the room, dragging her kids with her.

That was when we attacked him.

* * *

The waitress took the woman and children to a private room where hot meals and large cups of hot cocoa awaited them.

"There are clean, warm clothes on the counter." She had to shout to be heard over the din of the ruckus outside the door.

The woman nodded, and the children smiled. They would soon be free.

"You're part of our family now. Mama Bernadette provides us with jobs and housing." The waitress crouched down before the kids and hugged them. "Nobody's ever gonna touch you, hurt you, or scare you again. You'll come here every day for meals and comfort."

Then she handed several business cards to the woman. "Pass these around when you can. You'll know who needs them. We all seem to have that intuition."

The woman regarded the cards, all stamped with the same message:

Mama Bernadette's
We're off the beaten path
To serve your man his just desserts
For reservations:
www.mamabernadette.org

I, myself, still have a few of these cards left in my purse.

SOMEONE TO WATCH OVER ME

Elizabeth,
I have your Physics notes.
(You know, the ones of which you have no copy?)
To claim what is yours, two tickets to the Winter Dance will be needed.
Put the tickets in the Table of Contents of *The Catcher in the Rye* found on the Librarian's desk by 2:30 p.m. today.
Your physics notes will be returned to you immediately following the drop-off.

Elizabeth leaned against her locker and stared at the type-written note once more. Extra tickets to the high school dance were non-existent. Even she didn't have any. The Social Events Committee had run out during the first twenty minutes of the sale. Still, she needed those physics notes desperately because next week's college placement exam was heavily weighted in that area. Her scribblings were useless to anyone outside of her scholar's program.

Could it be someone from her class who did this? Elizabeth mentally scrolled through the list of girls and shook her head. It didn't seem likely. Nerdy girls are competitive academically, true, but none of them were aggressive enough socially to demand dance tickets. But, before she could solve this, she had better get two of those elusive dance tickets.

On her way to Study Hall, Elizabeth stopped by the Social Events office. Sitting at the desk was Patricia McKenzie, captain of the cheerleaders, AKA Pom-Pom Patti. Fluttering her heavily made-up lashes and smiling brightly, Patti acknowledged her. "Hi, Lizzie! What can I do for you?"

Oh, how I hate this, thought Elizabeth. *Why can't she call me Elizabeth like everyone else? She knows I hate nicknames.*

Mirroring Patti's enthusiasm, Elizabeth spoke up. "Hey, Patricia, there's a rumor going around school that there might be some dance tickets stashed away. Of course, when I heard that, I refused to believe it. After all, we are all young ladies of virtue here at St. Julia-Child of God, right?"

Elizabeth leaned over the desk, closing in on the startled cheerleader/committee chairperson. "If—and I'm saying 'if'—such a rumor were true, what would a person have to do to save your pom-poms, Patti?" This was a bluff, but Elizabeth had a hunch she was right.

Patti regained her composure, strained her neck to see if anyone was within earshot, and whispered, "I might have a pair left. Maybe they were misplaced during the sale. I can get them for you–in lieu of a favor. Are you in?"

"Talk to me."

"Well, you know Acne Andrea?"

"Andrea Terranova? Yes, she's the new girl in my calculus class. Her skin condition is due to severe allergies. Why?"

"Whatever. Sister Renee Sans Faire has appointed me to be her mentor, and she needs a date for the dance. Get her an escort and the tickets are yours."

Elizabeth sighed. In a way, she was glad to be missing this fiasco. There was too much on her plate, both in school and at home. She had no time for such nonsense. "Okay, let me see what I can do. Give me an hour. I'll meet you here."

She just made it into Study Hall when the bell rang. Elizabeth slid in her seat beside her clueless but cute best friend, Jenna Saykwa. "Psst, Jenna, is your cousin still visiting you?"

Jenna paused for a moment to process the question and nodded. "He sure is. My mother is making me take him to the dance instead of Gordon. What a drag, all because 'He's our guest and he loves to dance. It's the right thing to do, Jenna.'"

"I have a brilliant idea. Would he be willing to go to the dance with Andrea? Everything is paid for already. All he has to do is just take her. Then you're free to go with Gordon."

Elizabeth waited patiently for Jenna's response. She was a great and loyal friend, but the Saykwas were always a little slow on the uptake.

"I have to call him. Give me a minute." Jenna raised her hand to be excused and winked at Elizabeth as she left the room.

During that time, Elizabeth tried to recall as much of her Physics notes as she could. She wrote furiously while anxiously watching the door for Jenna's return. Finally, her BFF walked through the door, beaming.

"Well?"

"What?"

"What did your cousin say?"

"He said my dress for the dance just arrived. I'm so excited. I was worried that it wouldn't get here on time, but now I'm relieved—"

Elizabeth snapped her fingers, "Hey, focus, Jenna, focus. Did you ask your cousin about taking Andrea?"

"Oh, that. He said okay. He loves to dance so much he'd be willing to go with our principal, Sister Bernoulli."

In her head, Elizabeth was doing cartwheels and shouting for joy.

Immediately after Study Hall, Elizabeth ran back to the Events office. Patti was there, tapping her foot and looking at her watch. Handing her a piece of paper, Elizabeth said, "Here you go, Patricia. The name, address, and phone number of Andrea's date for the dance. His name is Anton Saykwa. Now, please, may I have those coveted tickets?"

Patti handed over an envelope. "Remember, the Events Committee does not ever put tickets on the side for friends or bribes."

"Oh, of course not." Elizabeth nodded innocently. "We are young ladies of the highest standard here at St. Julia-Child of God."

* * *

Checking the hallway clock, Elizabeth, rushed to the library. She put the two tickets in the book as instructed by the ransom note, sat down, and looked around her. She didn't have long to wait and was totally surprised at the person retrieving the book.

"You seem shocked, Elizabeth." Sister Rosetta, her Language Arts teacher, said as she sat down at the table. "Your boyfriend is quite a persuasive young man. He called the school and explained the circumstances that led to you missing the ticket sale. He's been watching you closely and noticed you've been swamped with your pre-college courses, working at your mother's store, and taking care of your ailing grandmother. You really have had no time for yourself, up all night studying, rising early to get to school. It didn't seem fair to him, and I agree."

"So, the tickets are not the ransom for my physics notes?"

Sister Rosetta chuckled. "No dear, your notes are safe in Sister Rae Diashon's office. You left them in her class when you rushed out yesterday."

"I still don't understand. The tickets were sold out. I heard the announcement."

"It's true. However, we always keep a pair of tickets as an incentive or reward for an outstanding student. That would be you."

"Was this some kind of ploy?"

"No, no, my child. Andrea did need a date, and you would never make an effort to get tickets for yourself." Sister Rosetta took Elizabeth's hand. "Do not burn out at such an early age. You're only 17, too young to be spreading yourself so thin. Take time for you. Enjoy life. It's our policy here to form well-balanced students at St. Julia-Child of God."

"Thank you, Sister. For once, I'm speechless." Elizabeth got up to leave.

"Enjoy the dance. Your young man, Benjamin, said that he watches you every day, is always nearby and wants to take care of you. In fact, he's probably waiting outside for you right now."

Elizabeth froze in her tracks. Benjamin? Benjamin who? Her boyfriend's name was Nick!

STILL CRAZY AFTER ALL THESE YEARS

Both of my roommates think I am insane, but what do we accept as normal? How far would you go to appear sane to others? I went as far as a college in another state. Maybe I went too far.

I came to this university from South Brooklyn, a girl of the streets. When the two other girls in my dorm and I introduced ourselves to each other, we shared some of our life stories and experiences. To the pedigreed pair, my past was not considered 'par for the course'. Wendy Wasp and Sarah Snoot sat on their beds and peered at me through long fake lashes.

"You did what? Played Skanky?" Wendy was wide-eyed.

"No, I said I played Skelly. It's a game with bottle caps in a chalk-drawn square in the center of the black-tarred streets."

"Sounds exciting." Sarah suppressed a yawn as she got up to unpack her Louis Vuitton luggage.

"Okay, ladies, tell me what you did for fun while growing up." It was my turn to feign interest.

"Oh, shopping, spas, going to the club." Wendy counted out these activities on her well-manicured fingernails.

"Clubs? I went to clubs. Odyssey, The Tap Room, The Electric Circus, and The Café Wha? My friends and I would try to persuade an adult to buy us a bottle of vodka to mix with our own orange juice. We drank screwdrivers and boogied until closing time." I reminisced while thinking about how much I really missed my friends back home.

Wendy broke my reverie. "I was talking about Club Supercilious, the country club of the truly condescending. You know, where the elite golf, play tennis, or read magazines by the pool."

Sarah perked up and joined the conversation. "I thought you looked familiar. I remember seeing you there, Wendy. Who's your favorite lifeguard? I like Brent. He's dreamy."

I had to turn away so neither of my roommates could see my expression of disgust.

"Oh, no, I like Wimbly–his eyes are as blue as the spa's Jacuzzi," Wendy sighed.

Wendy and Wimbly? Now I was gagging.

"Do you have a beau, Jessica? Someone you like to be with when you're not playing in the streets?" Sarah giggled as Wendy spoke.

"Yeah, as a matter of fact, I do. And he's so dreamy, I can only see him when I sleep. His eyes…his eyes are as empty as an abandoned mine shaft."

Both girls blinked in confusion. I was elated.

"What's his name?" inquired Wendy the Wealthy.

"I'm not sure. Oh, I've been to several séances and psychics to communicate with him, but he never gives his name when we make contact."

"You mean he's not real?" breathed Sarah the Spoiled.

"He might have been real at one time in some long-ago era. Who knows? I can describe every feature of his face except for his eyes. They're just… not there."

The girls shivered in fear at this revelation. As far as I was concerned, mission accomplished. Wait. Maybe not. Perhaps I should add a cherry to the crazy cake I had frosted with the paranormal.

"One psychic told me that he's not just in my dreams. His spirit follows me around everywhere I go. Maybe we were connected in a past life." I pointed to a corner of our dorm room. "Can you feel his presence?"

My roommates were totally terrified. Speechless and clinging to each other, they crab-walked towards the door.

"Okay, okay. I was just kidding you. I have no country club stories or lifeguard love interests. So, I made this all up. You can relax now, ladies."

* * *

Both of my roommates think I'm insane, and that's good. There is no more girly, meaningless chit-chat in our dorm. They tip-toe around me and make no sudden moves. Their haughtiness has disappeared and they do my bidding, fearing that I might conjure up an unwanted spirit.

I like living the dorm life. My only problem is diverting my roommates' attention from the unexplained sliding and floating objects. Coughing does drown out the sudden thuds and bumps, but not the moans.

After all, I promised these girls that my ghost story was fiction and that I was joking. But was I? Only my phantom friend and I know the real answer!

TELL HER ABOUT IT

Robin was a very clever girl in many ways. Even at five years old, she knew the value of a promise. As a child, she was frugal, saving the coins she found on the beach or in the park. One time, her brother, whom she adored, wanted to borrow a dollar from her. Although he assured her he would repay her, Robin asked him to give her something he cherished to hold onto until she got her dollar back.

"A promise is a promise," she reminded him.

When Robin grew up, she pursued a law degree and graduated at the top of her class. Many prestigious firms contacted her, but Robin chose to be a Public Defender. She was fluent in four languages, an advantage in this field. Her reputation as a ruthless PD was stellar. Prosecutors feared Robin, while criminals worshipped her.

* * *

"Hey, Jerry, listen to me. Jerry, you gotta ask for this chick to defend you. She never loses." The two young men sat at the police precinct, handcuffed to chairs, thinking about their imminent fate.

"I dunno, man. This is bad. Really bad." Jerry shook his head sadly.

"No, I swear she's good. She got my cousin Michael off with no time served. It's like she's magic or somethin', y'know?" Charlie could be very persuasive.

"How do I get her?"

"Let me think." Charlie scratched his head with his free hand. "You got rights. You tell them that you don't speak good English and you need someone who speaks your language. The cops will bring her to you. They always call for her. You don't even have to know her name."

"You sure?"

"Yeah. You can ask my cousin, Michael. If you can find him. He disappeared right after he was let go. Who knows where he is now?"

Jerry looked up from his seat and called to the arresting officer, "Hey you! I need a public defender, but I got a language problem."

* * *

"So tell me, honestly, are you guilty? Did you do what the cops say you did? Don't lie to me." Robin looked intently at Jerry from across the table in the interrogation room.

Jerry stared at the petite blonde, debating whether or not he should tell the truth. "Yeah, I did it. You can see it on video. It's probably all over the internet by now. You got to be one hell of a lawyer to get me out of this."

She waved her hand as if to dismiss his statement. "Don't worry about the video. For every incriminating capture on film, there's another contesting one in cyberspace. Let me worry about that."

He sat back in his chair, slightly more relaxed than before, but still worried. Jerry was sure that he would spend a long time behind bars. *How was she gonna convince a jury that he was innocent of murder?*

* * *

"Ladies and gentlemen of the jury, if you examine the video closely, you'll notice that the killer's face is not discernible at all. In addition to my client, how many people fit the physical features of the person in the video? Look around this courtroom and you'll see several right here. Could you presume that any one of them is guilty of this murder?"

Robin leaned in closer to the jury, "This is a grainy low-resolution film that is not continuous. It appears to be edited. Any intelligent person would question the validity of using this as evidence."

Her banter, knowledge, and charm always swayed the jury in her favor. However, there was another reason why she never lost. Robin and her staff would stay up nights going over testimonies, reviewing evidence, searching for loopholes, or slip-ups that might have occurred during the arrest or investigation. She was definitely the prosecutor's nightmare.

* * *

Jerry hugged his family and stuck his tongue out at the victim's family. He was free! A minor technicality had released him from a guilty verdict and serving time in prison. *This bitch is the best and she didn't cost me a penny.*

He showed no remorse for his actions and didn't even thank Robin. *Par for the course,* she thought. *They never say thanks because they don't care about anyone else.*

* * *

Sipping her glass of Cabernet Sauvignon, Robin looked up to see the waiter approaching.

"I'm sorry to interrupt your dinner, madam, but a young man informed me that you dropped your wallet."

She studied the expensive designer wallet and held out her hand to receive it. "Why, thank you, sir. I would've been lost without it."

Robin opened the wallet, counted the bills, smiled, and read the enclosed card: "Thank you for all your help." This note of gratitude was appreciated but not necessary.

83

The family of the victim had been guaranteed that Jerry would no longer be a threat to anyone, anywhere, anymore. Robin's 'staff' had taken care of that.

This time the video recording of Jerry was so clear there would be no doubt as to his identity as he was executed.

She was a great public defender. As long as you admitted your guilt, Robin could get you off, but there was a higher price to pay: the perpetrator's life for a handsome fee paid by the victim's relatives.

Ever since the death of her brother, she promised to punish his killer and others like him. Her beloved brother was lying in a grave while his cold-blooded killer, Michael, enjoyed working out at the prison gym, conjugal visits with his favorite females, and other perks from the inmates. She offered to appeal his case, knowing she would win, thus setting him free. From that point, it was easy to avenge her brother's death.

Still, Robin had a criterion as a public defender:

1. Approach the victim's family and explain your strategy.

2. Make sure your client admits to being guilty, but shows no regrets.

3. Win your case. No problem there–her staff was ruthless. They paid off witnesses and jury members, tampered with evidence, and erased segments of videos.

4. Employ your minions to carry out justice.

5. Collect your legal fee, although she would have gotten revenge for free.

Yes, Robin was a clever girl in many ways.

THE MAN IN THE MIRROR

After closing on the house, the former owner, an elderly lady, asked, "Can I leave a few things here until I get help transporting them, my dear?"

"Of course, no problem." Four simple words that would haunt Jessica for the rest of her life.

One of the items left behind was a mirror in an ornate gilded frame. In spite of its size, it was light enough to be moved from room to room as Jessie and Steve worked on their newly-purchased home. In the next few months of remodeling, it became part of their restoration process.

"Why don't we just put it in the garage?" That was Steve, so practical.

"Oh, I don't know. As we move it around, the mirror seems to give us a different perspective of each room." Jessie sighed. "But you're right. Into the garage it goes." When she lifted it, she didn't notice that the reflection no longer coordinated with her surroundings.

In the garage, Jessie leaned the mirror against a dilapidated table, so it pointed towards her spacious backyard. It was then that she noticed a change in the mirror's image. A young girl, about six years old, was bent over the path which stretched from her kitchen door to the garage.

Flanking the small child was a man clad in a sweater and tie and a woman wearing a housecoat, her hair up in a bun. Both adults watched as the child wrote something in the wet cement. Jessie cautiously turned her head from the mirror toward the path.

Scrawled in the path was the name Lois 1961.

Did I just watch that happen? How is this possible?

Jessie studied the mirror again. Sure enough, the trio was still there. This time, the father picked up the little girl and swung her up on his shoulders. The mother was trying to clean the child's hands by dabbing at them with a rag.

This is so Norman Rockwell, yet eerie at the same time.

Jessie swiveled the mirror away from the yard. Staring at the back of it, she breathed slowly and counted to ten. Once again, Jessie pivoted it back to face her and peered into its silvery depths. She saw her house, but not the house she knew.

The image depicted the building as barn red, instead of the dove grey it was now. There was neither a back porch nor flowering cherry tree. Yet, Jessie observed the same man and woman as before. She was measuring the yard while he carried a small potted tree. Nearby, a little blonde baby watched from her playpen. *Those must be the original owners.* Jessie was mesmerized by the motion inside the mirror.

Suddenly, she got a crazy idea. *What if this mirror showed all the past activities of the house? I could find out how the mantles were installed and what the wood looks like under all this paint.*

Jessie lugged it back into the house. Thank God Steve had gone out to buy more paint. The last thing she needed was more of his criticism.

Positioning the mirror to face the dining room wall, Jessie gazed into it. After several minutes, she was about to give up when she spotted it. The dining room wall wasn't there anymore; in its place was a picture window looking out over the vast expanse of the yard.

I knew it. I knew there should've been a window there. It didn't make sense to have all that ornate molding just end and begin again five feet away.

She was smug before she witnessed what was happening. This time, the same couple stood by the window discussing something heatedly. There were tools strewn all over the floor. The woman appeared extremely angry, and the man held out his hands in resignation. Jessie was fascinated as the scenario played out. *Whatever they're saying can't be good.*

The man folded his arms across his chest and shook his head as if to convey his final act of disagreement. As he began walking away, she saw the woman pick up a hammer and strike his head several times. Jessie watched in horror as he crumpled to the ground.

Oh, my God! Time to turn this thing away from me. Who's gonna believe this? Even I can't process what I saw. Like an addict, unable to resist the dangers of a drug, Jessie turned the mirror to face her and the wall behind her. Now she saw only the woman, wearing a pleated smock and kerchief, painting the freshly plastered wall which once held a beautiful picture window.

No! It can't be. There's got to be another reason for blocking up the view.

She decided to call the old woman and ask her for more details about this particular renovation.

"Hello?"

"Um… hi. My name's Jessica. A few months ago, I bought a house from Katie Alexander. This is the contact number she gave. May I speak to her, please?"

There was a long pause before Jessie heard, "I'm sorry to tell you that Katie passed away two weeks ago. This is her daughter, Lois."

Now Jessie felt frustrated. "Well, I have her wall mirror. She left it here and promised to return for it. Would you like me to bring it to you?"

Jessie thought that Lois had hung up until she heard, "I can't talk about it now. But if I could, I'd tell you to get rid of that thing … please. For your sake and everyone else's."

An abrupt click left Jessie listening to a deafening silence. She ran to the mirror and smashed it with a kick to the center. Jessie continued to kick at the silver glass until only tiny shards littered the floor. Satisfied, she went to the bathroom sink to wash the perspiration from her face.

Looking at her reflection in the medicine cabinet mirror, Jessie dried her hands and brow. She told her image, "I'm not gonna dwell on the past of this house or mine, either. From now on, I'll only be looking towards the future."

Unfortunately, the bathroom mirror faced the front door of her house. Had she lingered just a moment longer in front of it, Jessie would have witnessed a car barreling down the street towards her.

Distraught and distracted, she left the house to walk off the experience and clear her head.

UNFORGETABLE

Giggling, gossiping, and ghost stories were the norm of Lena's pajama parties; but after one specific night, those girls would forever sleep with one eye open.

They sat cross-legged in a circle with Lena holding a flashlight. She dimmed the bedroom lights and positioned the beam under her chin, appearing ghostlike. "Listen up," she whispered, "this house is truly haunted. There's a presence here. Can you feel it? No? Not yet? Be still, listen, and maybe you 'll hear it."

A bouncing sound emanated from the ceiling; in the corner of the room. It didn't sound like a rubber ball, but an old fashion wooden ball.

"Who's doing that?" asked Maria, "is that your brother upstairs?"

"No, not my brother, but I have an idea." Lena aimed the flashlight at the ceiling. "It's always in that spot about this time every night. So I did a little research on the history of this house.

"Let's go upstairs; the room is empty right now. Mom's last boarder didn't stay long — maybe a week. Nobody lasts in that room for very long."

The girls followed Lena as she climbed up the stairs of the brownstone and tiptoed into the vacant furnished room. Lena panned the flashlight over the room, creating dancing shadows on every surface. It was eerily silent, Lena continued her story

"This house is almost 200 years old. Entire families would reside here and raise their kids; cousins, uncles, aunts, everyone under one roof. They all lived, died, and were waked in this house. You saw the cut out in the wall at the top of the stairs, right? That was so the corner of the coffin would not hit the wall as it was carried down to the street.

"People weren't so healthy back then, and some died at a very young age younger than we are. There was a little boy about seven years old who used to play with a wooden ball. He would roll it into blocks like a bowling ball, toss it in the air and catch it, or spin it around his other toys. He always had that ball with him. It was his favorite plaything. One year, after a bad winter, he caught pneumonia and was confined to his bed until the end of his life

"Knowing he wasn't going to survive, he asked his mom to bury his ball with him. Through her tears, she promised him. He smiled as he took his last breath. At that moment, his small hand slipped off the bed and released the ball he was clutching. It hit the floor with the thud, continued to bounce itself out, then rolled away. The boy's mom searched but never found her son's favorite toy."

Lena took a breath for dramatic effect. "That poor boy was laid to rest without the wooden ball he loved." Lena's friends were wide-eyed and speechless, afraid to move or look around the room. They focused their attention on Lena. She was not finished.

"So every night, at about this time I hear the sound of a wooden ball hitting the floor and bouncing itself out." Lena looked around at the girls and shrugged.

"Are you putting us on?" Jen sounded doubtful.

"No, I'm serious." I wanted to show you what's going on here. No one rents this place or stays long when they do. As her flashlight flickered and died, a glowing mist formed by the bed. Even Lena was alarmed by the sight.

From the mist, a soft, childlike voice eerily addressed the group. "She's telling the truth, you know. And it happened in this very room."

WHAT'S NEW PUSSYCAT?

Vicky looked up from the paper she was reading. *It's almost 2 a.m.! Where did the time go?* Her movement roused the gray tabby sleeping on the table next to a stack of unread papers–articles from journals all related to her thesis.

Vicky absently ruffled his fur. "Oh, Webby. Why did I sign up for this program now? I have plenty of time to get my Master's Degree. But, no, I had to hurry, hurry, hurry. I'm always rushing into things without thinking of the consequences."

"Mer-wow," Webby commented.

"There's so much here to sort out, and I've spent a lot of money copying all this research. I still don't know what to choose or where to start."

The cat blinked his eyes, stared at her, and muttered, "Merwow, wow, wow."

"Yeah, that's easy for you to say, but it's hard for me to present any instructional proposal in an order that makes sense."

"Wow." Webby seemed more alert as he lumbered his fat furry body closer to her. "Wow."

Vicky studied her feline friend intently before whispering, "It's almost as if you're trying to tell me something."

"Wow." Webby shook his head and strained his neck. "Wow… you… talk… a… lot."

Vicky's eyes widened. *I'm hallucinating! My brain must be melting away from breathing the toner fumes from the Xerox machine.*

The cat nudged her arm with his head. "What are you thinking? That I can't talk? Do you believe that all we cats do is just listen? Well, we do listen and form our own opinions about our human companions." He took a breath. "When we howl at night, that's our group therapy. But I can't take this anymore."

Webby lowered himself back on the table and crossed his paws in front of him. "Like I said, 'Wow, you talk a lot.' You think a lot, but you don't do a lot. When it comes to writing a paper, you have as much skill as a dead mouse." He looked around and surveyed the heaps of paper covering the dining room table. "Instead of talking, get cracking. You've discussed this so much out loud, that even I could probably write a thesis for you. But you know that's impossible. I can't hold a pen." He held up a paw. "No thumbs."

Vicky was dumbfounded. She couldn't speak, not even to answer her beloved pet. She watched him in fascination as he pulled papers with his teeth from the various piles and used his nose to push them in front of her.

"Check this out." Webby had his paw on the top paper. "This study is my favorite. It was proposed but never completed. Read it and commit it to memory. Rewrite this abstract in your own words. Update the theory to fit this decade and then get me a saucer of some warm milk, please. Not that low-fat kind, either."

Vicky read the article on an innovative method of teaching. The author had not finished proving his hypothesis due to his untimely death by his own hand. Although his philosophy was taught for generation after generation, no one ever took up the gauntlet to continue his study. *It could work,* she thought. *I can do this.*

Her eyelids felt weighted with fatigue, forcing her to stop reading and call it a night. Once again, she ruffled her tabby's fur as she got up to get him some milk.

"Thank you, Webby. You may have saved my career. I'm amazed you know so much about this approach to teaching."

The cat looked up at her, almost grinning. "Of course, this material you'll be using for your thesis will lay the groundwork for the application of logic in many other subject areas. By the way, please stop calling me Webby. I truly do not like that name.”

“Do you have a better name in mind for yourself?”

“When I was in human form, many centuries ago, I answered to the name of …Socrates.”

Vicky sputtered. “You? You’re Socrates? The great Greek philosopher? Isn’t this your theory I’m writing?”

As Vicky waited for a reply, the cat stretched, leaped off the table, and padded into the kitchen. He halted briefly to wash his face with his paws and looked back at her. His only response was…

“Mer-wow.”

WHO LET THE DOGS OUT?

After running for what seemed like hours, they stopped to hide behind a gnarled leafless tree. Very quietly, they took inventory of each other as they tried to catch their breath. With faces scratched by bare branches and shoes muddied from the muck and mire, they slid down to the cold damp ground.

"Did you see them?" she whispered.

"I saw what they did to Tommy. Poor bastard didn't stand a chance," he replied.

"Where did they come from? Where did they go?" She looked around the dark woods wild-eyed.

"Who are they? Can they hear us?" He peered around the tree trunk using the full moon's light as his only illumination.

"We need a plan," she said, "and a weapon. Something heavy enough to stop them and, you know, take them down."

"What we need right now is to be quiet. Just listen. They don't walk. They shuffle. We can hear them coming if you just shut up!" he hissed.

She put her hand over her chest as if she could slow the rapid beating of her heart that way. She thought that her pounding heart must be audible. Then they heard the sounds approaching.

The steady, erratic shuffle of leaves was slowly, yet ominously, nearing their flimsy hideout. Quickly, they looked around for anything they could use to stave off the inevitable attack, if only for a little while. He hefted a large fallen branch in swing position, like a homerun hero, ready to fight for their lives. She held a lighter but equally lethal-looking limb, moving her lips in silent prayer. In the distance, they could see those things seeming to come closer to them. A barking dog was heard in the background.

"Cut!" The young, bearded man jumped out of his chair and wiped his brow as he adjusted his baseball cap. "Winona, why is your mongrel loose on my set?" He looked around in exasperation at his crew. "Which of you idiots was supposed to watch Winona's flea-bitten mutt? Let's take five and get that animal outta my woods before he marks my territory. Hey, you zombies over there. Do not mess up your special effects faces. Our make-up girl went home sick after creating your ugly mugs."

After the break, everyone reconvened on the set. "Okay, is that doggone pooch secure now? Back to your positions, everyone. Winona, Brad, I want you to take it from the part where you're swinging the Styrofoam logs. Resume your places."

A ponytailed, gum-chewing girl walked up to the front with the clapboard yelling, "Zombie Babes in the Woods, take 666."

"And …ACTION!"

Miranda looked out from the diner's kitchen to the rows of empty checkered-cloth covered tables, nervously played with the buttons on her uniform, and shuddered. Something seemed wrong. She just didn't feel confident enough to voice her fears to the new waitress, Angela.

"Miranda, may I be honest with you?" Angela was wrapping the cutlery in the crisp white napkins. "You seem aloof, cold, almost like you've built a wall between yourself and humankind. All I said was that I wanted to get to know you better."

Putting down the half-filled sugar container, Miranda turned to Angela. "I appreciate you trying to get closer to me. After all, we do work together, but I can't chance any more good friends. I've lost so many in the past six years, I'm starting to believe I'm the Doctor Kevorkian of friendships."

"Do you want to talk about them? Would it help if you opened up to me?"

Miranda sighed, "I don't know." She glanced at the wall clock. "Well, maybe we do have some time before we open."

She sat down, filled more sugar containers, and began her synopsis of dearly departed friends. "First, there was Joann. We met in 1984 and formed an unbreakable bond over the next twenty years. Oh, we were two wild and crazy moms. The 'Thelma and Louise' of the Northeast.

"Once we attended a PTA meeting at someone's house, the door was unlocked, and we were halfway up the stairs before we realized we were in the wrong house! The pictures on the wall look nothing like the PTA president or her family. We would give unsolicited advice to young couples, or break out in song and dance in the middle of the street for no reason.

"She died in 2004 of lung cancer. Even in her last days, she still kept her sense of humor: she kept moving her morphine patch around her body so that her husband could play 'Where's Waldo' just to keep things interesting. I do miss her. She was the Yin to my Yang."

Angela kept her eyes down and said, "Tell me about the others."

"Next, there was Grace, a science and computer teacher. She was quick-witted and quicker to volunteer wherever help was needed. She and I, and a few other friends, would meet once a month for dinner. Not here, of course.

"We would let down our hair and exchange stories about our jobs, the people we encountered, and the smart retorts we really should have said. Grace loved to travel, but I couldn't afford to accompany her. I'm sorry I didn't go at least once.

"She died unexpectedly in 2005 while snorkeling in Ecuador. Her heart, I was told. It took two weeks to get her body back to the States. In spite of my grief, I did give a kick-ass eulogy. It wasn't that hard. Grace was indeed amazing."

Angela avoided her gaze, afraid Miranda might read her mind. She was not noted for having a poker face. "Who else?"

"Robin, my 'work sister'. We were reading the same book, *Bitch* by Jackie Collins. That alone brought us close. Through the years, we got so close that we could have complete conversations just by exchanging glances. Robin was a beautiful, intelligent black woman but with very low self-esteem. Rather than promote herself or brag about her accomplishments, she did much more to help others. Because of that, she had no time for doctors, even when she complained of not feeling 'in the pink.'

"After much prodding, she finally went to the doctor, a specialist, who diagnosed her with diabetes. He recommended the amputation of some of her toes and told her to take it easy. However, Robin believed herself to be immortal. Oh, she was wrong, so wrong.

"In 2006, she died suddenly, on one of her days off from work. I miss her clever nicknames for everyone."

Angela concentrated on lining up the napkins. "Is that everyone?"

"No, there was also my cousin, Marie." Miranda's voice was beginning to crack with emotion. "She was a family outcast by association with me. My family wanted me to conform to their ways and constantly tried to stifle my creativity. Yet, Marie encouraged me to think outside the box, even to build a different type of box and think outside of that one! She gave me the confidence I needed to accept the non-approving attitude of my relatives. You couldn't get a better cheering section than Marie, no sir. Unfortunately, she passed away in 2007 of colon cancer. There went my fan club and a good buddy."

Angela turned to look out at the dining room, hiding her face from Miranda. *She must not know about me. Not yet, anyway.* "So, did you bury any more close friends?"

"Yes, three more within the next three years. One was Marion, the sweetest person you could ever know. We met at a seminar and found that our shared interest in coupon clipping kept us together. We were in the habit of snipping and exchanging magazine articles, catalog ads, whatever tickled our fancy.

"Marion joined our monthly dinner group and fit right in. Her positive demeanor betrayed her sad history. As a child, she had lost her brother, and in her teens, her parents. Then, in her adulthood, she lost her life-long companion. She was alone but never lonely. Marion kept busy with various charities, religious groups, and women's clubs. Unfortunately, throat cancer also offered to keep her company and quickly ended her life. Marion was like a butterfly, overcoming obstacles, and willing to change to achieve her goals. What a loss to humanity." Miranda shook her head and blinked back tears.

"I'll never forget Betty, the spry senior citizen who taught me that 81 was the new 25. She went to the gym five days a week. She loved shopping, attending the theater, and dancing. Once, she confided in me that she belonged to a motorcycle gang, and even rode her own motorcycle!

"In her heyday, she was a professional singer and dancer. What a woman and role model! When she was a young mother, her husband abused her. So she grabbed her two boys and hopped on a plane to Hawaii. Her rationale? 'Honey, there are battered women shelters everywhere–why not go to one with good weather and a great view?' It made sense to me.

"Finally, Louise, my friend for life. She was so delightful, that my mother used to introduce Louise as her daughter and me as the bad influence. If you eve saw the movie Gone with the Wind, you would understand that Louise could be Melanie Wilkes. We met as teenagers and I introduced her to my boyfriend's best friend. We married those guys and stayed in touch all those years.

Louise's lungs were failing her and she was attached to an oxygen tank 24/7. Sadly, she succumbed to her illness while waiting for a transplant. I guess God needs these loving souls, more than I do. Still, I miss every one of my good friends and the beautiful memories we shared."

Miranda stared at Angela. "You've been so quiet, and you haven't looked at me all this time. Have I upset you? Are you reconsidering becoming my friend?"

"No, not at all. I just think now is the time to be honest with you, Miranda. My full real name is Angela De Lamorte, which means Angel of Death. See? In the parking lot? Don't those cars look familiar? Like those of your good friends? Now, look at the tables in the dining area."

Miranda peered through the opening in the kitchen wall at the customers sitting down. They held the menus high to cover their faces.

When did everyone come in? What time was it? Was it time to serve? Who unlocked the door?

It was then Miranda saw the faces of her customers as each one lowered her menu: Louise, Betty, Marian, Marie, Robin, Grace, and Joann! All were dressed in cruise wear with brightly colored suitcases by their seats. Each woman wore sunglasses propped on top of their heads so that Miranda could see the twinkle in her friends' eyes. The women seemed so happy, very happy. Maybe too happy. Why?

Angela got up, walked over to Miranda, and touched her shoulder, making her gasp and jump.

"Don't be afraid, my friend. Sorry to say, but this morning you had a major heart attack right here in this kitchen. However, I'm happy to state that you are very loved and blessed. These women knew your time on earth was over, so they requested to escort you to your final destination.

"It's time to enjoy paradise with them. Here is your suitcase and your travel outfit. Many other souls are awaiting your arrival. Go with God, Miranda. He's waiting for you."

Miranda sighed once more, glanced at the crumpled body of the waitress on the floor, then turned and headed towards the door, towards the welcoming, bright light.

Acknowledgements

I THANK YOU

Putting this book together took a lot of time, not due to its difficulty, but because I tended to procrastinate

Now that this endeavor is done, I'm grateful to many people (living and dead) for their encouragement, ideas, and support.

My stories are inspired by Stephen King and O'Henry (if they had a child, it might have been me). I also thank Isaac Asimov, Ray Bradbury, and Wes Craven for possibly channeling their thoughts through my dreams. When George Romero died, I refused to sleep for quite some time! My only hope is that someday, Mr. Stephen King might read one of my stories and say, "Why didn't I think of that?" or "That would make a great movie."

Special thanks to Shonda Rhimes–every episode of her show, *Grey's Anatomy,* is a song title, thus leading to my 'Twisted Tunes of Terror'.

Thank you to my family and friends, who believed in me and enjoyed my insanity: the Royal Palm Beach Writers group, Dottie Littlefield (my role model), John Rifenberg (my "big brother"), Ginny Smythe (the "good" Virginia), Judith Pelio (my conscience), Margie Bonner and Gloria Ferarra (you started this), Don Conway (my father figure), and Hartley Barnes (who gave ice cream a new meaning).

Thank you, Ruth Sutton–you knew I could do this! Last but not least, my husband Ralph, who dared me to do it.

And thank *you*, dear reader. I hope you have enjoyed my book and look forward to more of my stories.

MEET VIRGINIA

Virginia Guido was born in Brooklyn, N.Y. and raised by her mother and grandparents. She married Ralph, her childhood sweetheart, in 1973. Her beloved son, Frankie, died in 2008. Her twin daughters (Natalie and Paulette) have blessed her with six grandchildren: three energetic grandsons (Jax, Gio, and Jet), one beautiful granddaughter (Gemma) from Natalie, and two exquisite granddaughters (Bianca and Juliana) from Paulette.

Virginia is a retired NYC school administrator, currently living in Florida. Because she was predominantly a science and math teacher, Virginia never had the opportunity to hone her skills in prose until her retirement. Upon settling in the Sunshine State, Virginia joined the Royal Palm Beach Writing Group. This writing group has become her family, and crafting stories has become her therapeutic support (which may not be as successful as she believes since most of these stories are straight from her dreams). She is an integral member of the group and is the final editor of their annual published anthology.

Virginia enjoys writing horror stories and memoirs about her eccentric childhood; she regards both as the same genre. She is fond of the weird and unusual because "I, myself, am weird and unusual." Considered an "Unreliable Narrator," she is someone who takes you down a comfortable path, only to spin you around and blow your mind.